The Sun Will Still Come Up Tomorrow

by

Cherie M. Fields

DORRANCE PUBLISHING CO., INC.
PITTSBURGH, PENNSYLVANIA 15222

ISBN: 978-1-4349-0320-4
Library of Congress Control Number: 2008941303

Printed in the United States of America

First Printing

For information or to order additional books, please write:
Dorrance Publishing Co., Inc.
701 Smithfield St.
Pittsburgh, Pennsylvania 15222
U.S.A.
1-800-834-1803
www.dorrancebookstore.com

Dedicated to my granddaughter Miranda for her never-ending encouragement and her love of books.

Chapter One

Megan stepped out of the hot Texas sun into the air-conditioned parlor of the Guest Ranch. As she looked around the room, memories came flooding in on her. This had once been her Grammy's home. Megan remembered spending much of the summer here and helping Grammy plan huge barbeques for all the neighbors. She had many happy times at this ranch. Megan had a sudden burst of sadness overwhelm her as she came back to the present and the realization that both Grammy and Grampy were gone now and her Aunt Carol had sold all the property, except this house and ten acres surrounding it.

"Plenty of time to think on serious matters once I'm settled in," she scolded herself.

Megan saw a tall, slender, middle-aged lady arranging flowers in a large gold-rimmed crystal vase at one of the tables. As she turned and acknowledged Megan with a nod of her head and a smile, a curl slipped out of her perfectly coiffed hair and came to rest in the middle of her forehead. Megan couldn't help laughing to herself. Her mother had often told her stories of her aunt, Carol, who strove to look as if she had just stepped out of a fashion magazine. However, Carol had one curl that refused to cooperate with this image and would always work itself loose at the most inopportune times.

Since Aunt Carol had left the ranch at the ripe old age of sixteen to go to New York City and become a famous model, she knew very little of Megan and had never seen any pictures of her. Megan had been instructed to remain incognito, so this suited her plan very well.

"Welcome to Tumbleweed Guest Ranch," Carol said as she set the vase of flowers in the center of the table and extended her hand to Megan. "I'm Carol Marshall, the owner and operator," she continued.

"Owner, my eye!" thought Megan, but she extended her hand and flashed Carol a dazzling smile as she said, "Hello, Carol. I'm Megan O'Hara."

"Oh, yes. I've been expecting you." Carol suddenly had a puzzled expression on her face. "Your fax didn't indicate how long you are planning to stay with us," she continued without drawing a breath.

"That's because I'm not certain how long I'll be staying. Is that going to be a problem for you?" asked Megan.

"Well it does make it rather difficult for me to make other reservations. This is a very popular resort, after all," Carol said rather smugly.

Megan knew the Guest Ranch was barely staying afloat and only had thirty guests the entire previous year, but she enjoyed the games people play and went along with Carol.

"Oh dear, of course you are right. How very thoughtless of me!" exclaimed Megan. "If I'm willing to pay in advance for the entire summer, with the understanding that if I am unable to stay that long I will forfeit all monies paid in advance, will that help your predicament?"

Carol couldn't hide the smile on her face although she tried. *"I wish Mama were here to see what a good businessperson I am,"* she thought. *"I don't understand why she always thought May had more sense than me! Nobody even knows where May is or what she's been doing all these years!"*

Carol had to physically shake herself to stop the bitter thoughts of her sister from obstructing her reasoning. She had important matters to handle and no time for such foolishness.

"I'm sure we can work out an arrangement to fit both our interests," she smiled at Megan.

As they made their way to the suite Megan would occupy, Megan had a hard time concentrating on Carol's small talk. Her mind kept caressing memories of her childhood in this old house. As they passed the spot where the door leading to the basement used to be, she noticed there was now a paneled wall there with an old cupboard taking up most of the space. This piqued her curiosity.

"Is there a basement in this house?" she inquired of Carol.

"It was boarded up years ago because of flooding," replied Carol. "We now have a modern storm shelter off the back patio," she continued. "Don't worry. If a storm should come up, I'll see that you get to safety."

"I see. That's very reassuring," mused Megan, wondering why the basement had really been boarded up. She knew there had never been enough rain in this area to flood a basement and besides, the basement had always been tight. Grampy had built it with his own hands to protect his beloved wife and daughters during storms.

"And the plot thickens," she laughed to herself.

Megan felt in her heart that this was a wasted trip, but she had undertaken it to fulfill her ailing mother's wish. May had been ill since Megan had been born, and, somehow, Megan felt responsible. She knew her mother had a heart attack before she married Megan's father, but she carried the burden of guilt on her slim shoulders just the same. After her father died from lung cancer, Megan became caretaker of her mother. She loved May living with her. They had so much fun together when May felt well. They had fixed up their little apartment together and had many a laugh while doing it. Combining both their tastes had proven quite hysterical at times with the result being a gothic-western affair. Even now Megan had to smile to herself as she thought of all the comments friends made when they visited for the first time.

Megan didn't know why May felt there was some type of foul play involved in Grammy's death, and May wasn't going to enlighten her any.

"Just go down and snoop around a bit," May had told her.

May had contacted an old friend who had been the sheriff at one time. Roy had since retired, but assured her that his "boy" would handle the situation discreetly and help Megan all he could in his capacity as the deputy sheriff. Megan wasn't too keen on depending on a "boy" to keep her safe if it came to that, but May had assured her it would be fine and she was in no danger.

After showing Megan around the rooms she would call home for heaven only knew how long, Carol departed telling Megan that supper would be at six o'clock sharp. Megan couldn't imagine eating that early since no one in New York ate before nine o'clock, but she said that would be fine and would strive to be on time.

As soon as Megan had unpacked, she took her cell phone out on her balcony, checked to make certain no one was within earshot, and called May.

"I'm settled in and everything has gone smoothly so far," she reassured her mother. "Guess what rooms I'll be occupying?" she asked with the enthusiasm of a small child.

May had not heard that excited lilt in her daughter's voice for so long that she felt the excitement, too.

"I don't know. Tell me. Tell me!" she exclaimed mocking Megan's enthusiasm.

"The suite Grammy always used for you and Daddy!" Megan replied with a laugh. "I feel just like a little girl again!"

After telling her mother about the basement and her plans to investigate the "flooding" story, Megan hung up and hurried inside to take a quick shower before supper. She didn't realize how tired she was until the relaxing water trickled over her head and down to her toes. As she lathered the lavender soap and began rubbing her tense muscles with the soft, velvety foam, she again let her thoughts drift back to her childhood and her loving grammy.

"Why would Mother think anyone would want to harm such a sweet, old lady?" Megan wondered.

Grammy had helped just about everyone in these parts in some way or another, and everyone loved her. It just didn't make any sense to her.

"Oh well," she said as she shook her head. "If there was any foul play, I promise you I will uncover it, Grammy!" she said out loud as she reached for the fluffy, pink towel hanging on the rack.

As she crossed the bedroom to the huge walk-in closet, she glanced at her watch that was lying on the nightstand by the bed. Her long, relaxing shower had cut into her dressing time, but she was glad she had done it. She felt ready to take on the world now. She had exactly ten minutes to dress, make herself presentable for her want-to-be-model aunt, and find her place at the table downstairs. She quickly grabbed a black mid-calf skort with a matching jacket and bright pink blouse to add a bit of color to her cheeks and hurriedly put them on. She was glad she had the foresight to have her heavy curls cut short before making this trip. She tied a bright pink ribbon around her curls to help keep them out of her face, applied makeup, and headed for the door, putting on her sandals between steps.

She left in such a hurry she forgot her watch and wondered how close it was to six o'clock as she raced down the hall to the staircase. Her question was answered just as she reached the staircase and heard the huge grandfather clock in the parlor begin its first chime. Just as she had done as a child, Megan decided to gain some time by sliding down the long banister to the stairs. As she came to a halt at the bottom, she was face-to-face with the most incredible man she had ever seen.

"Good slide," he congratulated her with a big grin and a mischievous twinkle in his eye. "Not many girls can land on their feet like you did," he continued teasingly. "In fact, I only know of one other one, and she used to come here to visit Grammy in the summer. Boy, could she slide down that banister and climb higher in a tree than anyone!"

Megan knew this gorgeous mass of manhood was referring to her, but she just couldn't seem to get past the twinkling blue eyes, black wavy hair, and the mouth that seemed to be permanently in a crooked grin. She was sure she would not have forgotten him had they ever met.

Suddenly, she realized he was holding out his hand to shake hers and had said something. She reluctantly broke eye contact and composed herself.

"Hello, I'm Megan O'Hara," she stated rather businesslike as she extended her small, slim hand to his.

"Hello, I'm Deputy Sheriff Troy Brown," he mocked her as his huge, tan hand engulfed hers.

Megan lowered her voice and inquired with large, disbelieving eyes, "Are you Roy Brown's 'boy'?"

Troy couldn't stop himself: he threw back his head and laughed the most contagious laugh Megan had ever heard. Before they knew it, they were both laughing hysterically, his hand still wrapped around hers. All the noise brought Carol and two other ladies from the dining room.

"I just knew that was your wonderful laugh," said an elderly, blue-haired lady as she caressed his arm lovingly. "You silly boy, you've kept us waitin' for supper. The salad's gettin' warm and the soup's probably cold!"
She acknowledged Megan in no way. It was as though Troy was the only one standing at the bottom of the stairs laughing wildly at some joke known only to him.

"This is Ethel Muntz," said Carol gesturing toward the seemingly shy, younger lady who stood in the background. "And this shark who has Troy in her jaws is her mother-in-law, Viola Jones. Ethel is Viola's son's widow, and Viola was Mother's dearest friend since they were young. They try to join us for supper 'most every Friday night. Troy, here, just comes around to flirt with Viola."
Megan made a mental note to try to get close to Viola hoping to gain some important information. She remembered Viola and Grammy spending much of their time together during her visits. Viola seemed to like Megan then, so maybe she could get on her good side again.

Troy slowly extricated his arm from Viola's vise-like grip and raised his arm, still holding Megan's hand in his, in the air making Megan feel as though she had just won a prizefight.

"This lovely lady is Megan O'Hara, everyone, and I would take it as a personal favor if yawl would make her feel at home here," Troy announced.

Megan could feel the heat starting in her neck and feared she would soon be in full blush. She hoped no one would notice, but she often turned bright red when embarrassed.

"You know Megan, Troy?" interrogated Carol. "However did you meet?" Carol was astonished and somewhat skeptical.

"We met last summer while I was on vacation in New York. As a matter of fact, I'm the main, if not the total, reason Megan chose to spend her vacation out here in the sticks."

That did it! Megan could now feel her entire face burning from the heat of embarrassment!
"Okay, how should I respond to a statement like that?" Megan thought frantically. It was the perfect alibi for them spending time together, but Troy had caught her by surprise, and she wasn't very good at lying, or ad-libbing, whichever this was.

"Enough about us. There'll be plenty of time to tell you all how Troy thinks he swept me off my feet," Megan grinned and winked at Troy as she playfully jabbed him in the ribs. "We've held supper long enough. The cook would probably like to get home to her own family sometime tonight," she added.

"Oh, my goodness! I completely forgot about supper in all the excitement and confusion!" exclaimed Carol. "Of course, you must give us all the juicy details later, Megan."
Carol flashed Megan a fake smile if Megan had ever seen one. She wondered what that was all about.

Supper was spent in pleasant conversation mostly about people whom Megan had no clue what part they may have played in Grammy's life. Between the laughter and gossip, Troy would reach over and give Megan's hand a gentle squeeze and smile warmly at her.
"What is he trying to prove? None of my real boyfriends ever gave me this much attention!" she thought.

As the dessert dishes were being cleared away, the conversation slowly died down. The huge meal, all the laughter, and friendly insults seemed to have taken their toll. Megan thought Viola was going to fall asleep and lay her head in her dessert. Ethel begged off for coffee in the parlor saying she needed to get her mother-in-law home. As Carol was seeing them to their car, Troy turned to Megan and told her to come out back to the garden with him. Megan didn't like the way he seemed to order her around, but right now she needed his help and knowledge, so she obediently followed him through the French doors to the patio. Once they were outside and the doors were closed, Troy reached for Megan's hand and headed down a graveled path away from the house. Megan came to a sudden stop and jerked her hand free of his. Her independent nature could tolerate no more of this behavior.

"No one is watching us now," she exclaimed. "You needn't hold my hand. And for what it's worth, I don't like being touched like you were touching me all during supper! I know you were putting on an act, but it made me very uncomfortable. Please refrain from doing that in the future!" she snapped.

Troy was dumbstruck by her actions and sudden outburst. He felt as awkward as a teenager on a first date and was sure he had been standing there staring at this beautiful but strange creature with his mouth gaping open.

As he regained his composure he replied, "I'm sorry I made you uncomfortable. It felt quite natural to me, but I will try to remember to admire you from a distance from now on."

Megan wasn't sure if he was making fun of her again or if he was being serious, so she chose to ignore his apology completely. As they walked side-by-side down the moonlit path, Megan found it more difficult to ignore Troy, however. She had dreamed of having an attentive suitor all of her life and of walking down tree-lined paths in the moonlight with him. She reprimanded herself for having such silly thoughts and reminded herself she was treading in dangerous waters. If she wasn't careful, she could easily fall victim to this charade and end up with yet another broken heart for all her trouble!

All of a sudden the path ended and tree branches met overhead blocking the light. Megan was abruptly pulled from her self-chastisement by the change. She felt frightened standing there in the darkness with a total stranger. What had she been thinking? She didn't even know if this man was Roy's "boy" or not. He had never answered her question but had just burst out in wild laughter. Sure, Carol and the other ladies acted as if he were the deputy sheriff, but, after all, they were strangers, too. Maybe they were all in this foul play together! Megan could feel her pulse begin to quicken, and she was wondering if she could find her way back to the house and her car when Troy suddenly grabbed her by both her arms.
Everything went black!

Chapter Two

When Megan regained consciousness, she was lying on a cool but hard bench under a tree. Her thoughts were cloudy and she kept her eyes closed trying to remember what had happened. All of a sudden, the image of Troy grabbing her came rushing back, and she sat straight up on the bench unsure if he were still there or not. She wasn't sure in her mind which would be worse … him being there or her being alone in the dark unsure which direction the house was. She could feel panic beginning and then a soft, soothing voice broke into her thoughts.

"You weren't kiddin' when you said you didn't like to be touched, were you?" Troy tried to say jokingly, but Megan caught a wisp of worry in his tone.

"Why did you grab me like that and scare me half to death?" she demanded.

"I wasn't sure you could see me, and I wanted you to know where I was. Before I could say anythin', you collapsed. I didn't mean to skeer you. I just wanted to point out that we could talk here without worryin' about bein' seen or heard. If we meet here at a certain time, I can come from the adjoinin' land, which I own, and no one will ever know we're meetin'."

Megan's eyes had adjusted to the darkness and she saw the wooden fence separating the properties. Troy's land had belonged to Grammy, too, when Megan was younger. She and Grammy had sat on this very bench, which Grampy had built, and sipped ice cold lemonade after their afternoon chores were done. It was always so cool here in the shade that neither wanted to leave. Grammy would tell Megan all about life during those times.

"Remember, Angel, no matter how bad things seem, the sun will still come up tomorrow," Grammy would say while patting Megan's knee.

She missed Grammy and longed to sit beside her and lean her head on Grammy's shoulder as she had then. She was glad it was dark and Troy couldn't see how misty her eyes had become.

Megan couldn't believe how emotional she had become since arriving at the ranch. She usually took pride in the fact that she kept her emotions in check and remained in control of every situation. She decided she needed to thoroughly analyze her reactions later, but soon. She swung her legs off the bench and patted the seat beside her as she cleared her throat and her mind.

"How often do you think we'll need to meet here?"

"I'm not sure, Megan. That will depend how quickly you uncover things. Some days you won't uncover any new information, but other days you may have hundreds of questions you need me to find answers for."

"Yes, that's true. I already have several questions that you could research for me," Megan grinned up at him. "Are you sure you're ready to take on the world with a scaredy-cat like me?" she asked.

"Megan, Grammy was like a grandma to me, too. I loved her very much. I will do whatever I can to help you learn the truth. I really hope your mother's wrong, but Dad said ever since he can remember, May's hunches were right ninety-nine percent of the time. Guess she got that from Grammy."

They both grew silent, each deep in their own memories, thoughts, and ideas. Megan reluctantly broke the peaceful silence as she came to a decision on how often they would need to meet.

"Carol said you come to supper most Fridays, so she will be expecting you to come at least then while I'm here since I'm so madly in love with you," Megan said coyly.

Troy cleared his throat as if to speak, but just nodded his head instead. Megan continued, "Is there any place I could hide a note down here, if I needed you in the meantime?"

"Yes," Troy said. "Grammy and I used to pretend she was kidnapped and was bein' held captive here. We would plan her rescue by leavin' each other notes."

Troy was now standing on the bench and tree branches hid his head. He extended his hand to Megan and said, "Look what we did to this tree."

Megan took his hand and stood by his side. She could see nothing, however. Then Troy took her hand and rubbed it across the rough bark of the tree's trunk. There in the center was what felt like a small, corded loop.

"Pull it," he said.

As Megan pulled the loop, a piece of the trunk dislodged revealing a cubbyhole. Megan felt as though she were a child again and was excited that her new friend had shared such a secret with her. She squeezed Troy's hand in her excitement and instantly felt the heat begin in her neck.

"Grammy and I worked for weeks makin' this hidin' place. We had to be very careful so as not to damage the tree's growth. No one else ever knew about this. You and I can leave each other notes here and rest assured they will never be found by anyone else, not even the gardener."

Megan replaced the door to their hiding place and carefully turned to sit on the bench again. "Tell me about the floods, Troy," she said uncertainly.

Troy looked confused and plopped down on the bench rather boyishly. "What floods? The closest we've ever come to a flood around here is the time Grammy's hired hand, Bob Benson, turned on the windmill and forgot to turn it off till the next day when he was supposed to turn it on again. Grammy was fit to be tied! Kept grumblin' about it for months and kept remindin' Bob how precious water is around here."

"How strange," replied Megan. "Is Mr. Benson still around here?"

"Yeah, but he's drunk most of the time. He and Grammy grew close after Grampy died. He kinda looked to Grammy like a mother, and he hasn't been able to handle her death very well, I'm afraid. He's pretty well stayed drunk for the last six months since her funeral."

"We will probably need to sober him up and talk to him at a later time. If he was that close to Grammy, he may have important information that no one else would know."

The two again fell into their own thoughts. Troy seemed to sense that Megan needed these quiet times to organize her thoughts, analyze all information, and store each piece in a slot in her brain.

"I understand how this lady ticks 'bout like I understand how my computer at work operates. Oh well, I know how to turn my computer on, and maybe in time I can learn how to turn her on," Troy thought hopefully as he studied the ground beneath his boots.

"Troy," Megan seemed to stammer over his name. "How did you know I visited Grammy in the summer? Mother could've told your dad that, but she wouldn't have known about me sliding down the banister or climbing trees."

"You don't remember me, do you, Megan?" Troy sounded a little hurt. "Maybe this will help your memory. Imagine a boy shorter than you with freckles and huge black-rimmed glasses who followed you around like a little puppy. Does that jog your memory any?"

"Hoot...was that you?" Now it was Megan's turn to be dumbfounded. She had dubbed him the nickname the first time she saw him because of the big round glasses. She wasn't sure she had ever been told his real name. Again, they both laughed till tears rolled down their cheeks as they relived some of their antics as children.

"Well, one mystery solved. Now back to the serious one," sighed Megan. "Can you tell me anything about the circumstances of Grammy's death? We weren't even notified until a month after the funeral and were given no details!"

"All I know is Grammy had never been sick a day in her life. Then one mornin' around eight o'clock, Carol called Doc Reed and said Grammy was deathly ill. Doc came out to the ranch and called an ambulance to take her to the hospital. I never heard what was wrong with her. About a month later, Viola called the Doc around four o'clock in the mornin' and said she thought Grammy was dead. Carol had gone to a party the night before and spent the night in town. Viola had stayed with Grammy. Doc came out to the ranch and pronounced her dead. No one was allowed to view the body at the funeral home, and the casket remained closed and locked. I snuck in one evenin' and tried to open the casket. I wanted to see Grammy one last time. That's when I discovered it was locked."

"Was an autopsy performed?" quizzed Megan.

"No, and I never saw the death certificate, so I don't know what Doc listed as the cause of death. Man, that all sounds mighty suspicious now. I wonder why no one questioned it at the time."

"If she died suddenly without any prolonged illness, I'm sure everyone just assumed it was an accident. You might go to Public Records at the courthouse and take a little peek at that death certificate if it won't raise any eyebrows. I don't want to draw anyone's attention until I figure out all this," Megan cautioned.

"I can handle that without any questions. I have to dig through all sorts of documents in my job."

"That's great!"

For the first time, Megan sounded hopeful, and Troy couldn't help feeling pleased with himself. He sat there in the dark smiling that lopsided grin while beside him Megan fell silent in her thoughts again.

When Megan spoke again, her thoughts had taken her down a completely different trail. "My partner contacted Carol's accountant, Mr. Bonner, and informed him our firm was performing an independent audit of Tumbleweed Guest Ranch's books at the request of Edna Gilliam's youngest daughter, May Stein. Mr. Bonner assured him that the books were all in order, and he would overnight them to him that very day. I studied those accounts for weeks before coming out here, and the ranch is not self-sufficient. It doesn't bring in near enough revenue to pay all the bills. Of course, I had no legal grounds to look at Carol's personal books, but I'm wondering how she keeps the ranch open and why. Can you shed any light on this?"

"None at all," replied Troy. "I honestly have never even thought about it."

"Well, I aim to find out!" declared Megan.
"So, why did you ask about a flood?"

"I'm sorry," Megan apologized, "my mind jumps from one thing to another. I asked Carol about the basement today, and, assuming I was afraid of Texas storms, she was quite frank with me. She said the basement under the house had been boarded up years ago due to flooding, but there is a storm shelter in the back by the patio. Why would she lie about that?"

"Maybe she was just repeatin' what someone else had told her. She had been away from here for years, yanno. She only returned a few months before Grammy died. You don't seriously think Carol had somethin' to do with Grammy's death, do you?"

Megan let out a sigh. "Not any more than anyone else. I don't know these people like you do, and I'm looking at everyone like they're guilty right now. Just listen to me! I sound just like a television show," she giggled. "What business does an accountant have doing this investigating, anyway?"

Troy reached for her hand and placed it in the curve of his arm. "Come on, Detective O'Hara. I'll walk you to the precinct before the inmates get suspicious," he chuckled.

Megan laughed at Troy's antics and told him of her plans to do some exploring the next day. Carol had mentioned going to town to get supplies, and she wanted to go to the beauty parlor, too. Megan hoped she would have the house and grounds to herself most of the day. She felt content on the walk back to the house. She was glad she had met her old friend Hoot after all these years, and she felt Grammy was in Heaven smiling down at them.

Chapter Three

As they approached the house, it appeared as though every light was out. Megan hoped she hadn't been locked out on her first night here. Troy kept walking and making small talk as though there were nothing to worry about, so she tried to calm her anxious spirit.

"Guess I kept ya out pretty late," Troy drawled. "Hope ya won't hold it against me."

"Not at all. It was…hmmm …. an interesting evening? Can't say I've ever been on a date quite like this one," Megan joked.

"Well, I'll be seein' ya." With that Troy bent and gave her a peck on the cheek and quickly disappeared around the side of the house.

As Megan entered the house, she saw that Carol had left the light above the stairs on for her. She knew the old house like the back of her hand and could've made her way to her room in the dark, but the light was welcoming. Megan couldn't resist the urge to study the wall behind the big cupboard. She rubbed her hands across every inch that the cupboard didn't cover. To her disappointment, it felt like a normal wall.

"What did you expect, a hidden passage?" she ridiculed herself. *"I need some sleep. I'm being silly,"* she concluded.

She tiptoed up the staircase in case Carol was sleeping nearby and was a light sleeper. She wasn't sure if she should leave the light on or not, but opted to turn it off as she headed for her own suite still thinking about the events of the day.

It was almost two o'clock in the morning by the time Megan finally crawled into bed. The sheets smelled like fresh mountain air and the comforter warmed her entire body. She had forgotten how cool it got here at night. She fell asleep quickly in spite of all the unanswered questions running through her mind.

The sun streaming in through her bedroom window awakened Megan. She couldn't believe she had slept so late. She normally rose early so she could watch the sunrise. She was sure she had missed breakfast, and Carol was probably fuming. She yawned and stretched and just wanted to lie there. Grammy's beds always made you feel as if you were in her arms, and, right now, Megan seemed to need that more than anything else. She was still fighting with herself about getting up when there was a soft tap at her door.

Megan sat up in bed and said, "Come in."

It was Agnes, the cook, carrying a beautifully arranged breakfast tray complete with a long-stemmed red rose in a crystal vase.
"Miss Megan, I thought you might be hungry, so I kept some breakfast warm for you," Agnes said as she flashed Megan a toothless grin.

"How very thoughtful of you!" Megan exclaimed as she reached for her watch to check the time. Only nine o'clock, which by New York standards was an acceptable time to rise.
Curiously she asked, "Does Miss Carol know you did this?"

Agnes' expression changed from fright to conspiracy.
"Oh, no, Miss Megan! 'Twould mean my job for sure and possibly my head on the choppin' block," she confided.

Megan had to withhold her laughter because Agnes looked serious.
"Don't worry, Agnes. This will be our secret," she said as she reached to pat Agnes' hand. Agnes abruptly moved her hand, smiled at Megan, and almost ran to the door.
"What curious behavior! I must remember to ask Troy about that." Just the mention of Troy made Megan wish he were there. She felt so safe with him by her side. *"Oh, you silly goose, you know you're safe. Fear is just an excuse to get Troy out here, and he has a job to do!"*

Megan took her tray to the table on her balcony and munched on the crisp country bacon and a piece of toast while she drank a cup of coffee. Her peaceful breakfast was shattered as angry voices rose from the garden path. She edged her way closer to the banister in hopes of seeing the perpetrators. They must've been in the trees because she couldn't see anyone; however, she could make out their words quite clearly.

"I'm telling you that you will do as I tell you, or you'll be looking for new employment by nightfall!"

Megan thought, *"That sounds like Carol, but who could she be talking to that way?"*

"And I'm tellin' you, missy … I don't care who ya think ya are … I won't do nuthin' that goes against what I believe is right! I ain't goin' to Hell for the likes of you!"

"A male voice, but who in the world can it be?" Megan mused.

Carol and a man Megan had never seen before emerged from the woods at that time. Apparently, they knew not to continue their conversation so close to the house. Carol continued toward the house as the man began pruning a nearby tree.

"We'll discuss that matter at a later date, Jake," Carol threw over her shoulder in the man's direction without turning around.

It appeared to Megan that the man made no attempt to answer her.
"I wonder what awful thing Carol is wanting Jake, the gardener, to do." Megan made a mental note to discuss the entire affair with Troy as soon as possible. She also needed to know Jake's last name.

She hurried into her room carrying her tray with her. She intended to dress and take it to the kitchen before Carol had a chance to discover it. All of a sudden, her bedroom door flung open and in marched Carol!
"Well, Miss Nosy Parker, did you get an earful from your balcony? I don't know what your story is, yet, but I guarantee you I will find out! I do not appreciate my guests, or anyone else, sneaking around spying on me!"

"Whatever are you raving about?" inquired Megan, looking childishly innocent. "I'm not spying on anyone, and I resent the accusation! I was simply enjoying the beautiful morning when I saw you and the gardener. I was going to wave to you, but you seemed to be discussing the tree pruning with him, and I didn't want to interrupt," lied Megan.

Carol seemed to have gained some control of her temper and became aware of the tray Megan was holding.

"Who brought you that tray so late in the morning, anyway?" Carol demanded.

"No one. I went to the kitchen and prepared it myself. I didn't know that was against the rules. I thought the whole idea of a 'guest' ranch was to make the guests feel at home. I was obviously mistaken!" retorted Megan.

"If this is the manner in which all the guests are treated, no wonder there are so few who come back a second time! This woman is either a lunatic or on some mighty strong drugs," Megan thought.

Carol's rage disappeared as quickly as it had appeared. She was now stumbling over her words trying to apologize and get in Megan's good favor. She didn't want Megan leaving before she had paid for the summer, and she sure didn't need any more degrading remarks made about the Guest Ranch! She tried to take the tray, but Megan wanted to let Agnes know she had protected her, so she told Carol to go on to town and she'd take care of the tray herself.

"Well, if you're sure. It would probably relax me to get my hair and nails done," Carol commented as she relinquished the tray.

After Megan saw Carol's car pull out of the driveway, she quickly brushed her teeth and dressed. She had much to do, and wasn't sure how long Carol would be gone. She gathered the tray, grabbed her watch, and headed for the kitchen.

Agnes was sitting at the table dabbing at her eyes with a paper towel. Megan rushed to her side to tell her Carol had no idea she had prepared the tray for her. Agnes looked up with a grin, and Megan realized Agnes wasn't upset at all … she was dicing onions. Megan sat down at the table and laughed as tears started to roll down her cheeks, too. She told Agnes what had transpired in her room and what she had thought when she entered the kitchen. The ladies laughed together and visited like they were lifelong friends.

"Is the gardener your son or some relation to you?" Megan asked after awhile.

"Oh, no, Miss Megan. The gardener is Jake Muntz. He's married to a friend of Miss Carol's."

"Jake is married to Ethel?" Megan asked astonished.

"Yes, ma'am. I don't think he likes Miss Carol much, though, 'cause they's always fightin'. He used to own his own land and forgets his place. Don't take Miss Carol long to put 'im back in it, though!"
Agnes let out a big sigh, got up from the table, and began food preparations at the counter. Agnes had dismissed her. Megan knew she'd get no more information from her at this time.

"I'm going to go out and admire the grounds till lunchtime. I've remembered to wear my watch, so I won't be late this time," she promised.

Megan could see Jake still pruning the trees as she stepped out on the patio. She stood there watching him for a while and then decided she didn't have enough insight about him to chance questioning him. Instead she turned and made her way toward the other side of the house keeping a lookout for what might be basement windows or an outside entry to the basement. She did not recall either from her childhood, but was hoping there were some. She did remember an old coal chute. She and Hoot used to climb inside it and play like it was their fort until Grampy caught them one day. He forbade them to ever play around such a dangerous place again. Fear of what Grampy would do to them, rather than fear of the coal chute, kept them away from it.

Megan had walked around the entire house and knew no more than when she'd begun. She couldn't help feeling somewhat disappointed, but she knew this was not going to be an easy task when she started it. She walked across the grassy landscape to the woods, which surrounded two sides of the house. Picking her way through the trees and dense undergrowth, she avoided the section where she had last seen Jake working. She wasn't sure what she hoped to find among the trees, but she was determined to look over every inch of the ranch looking for anything that would shed light on what had happened to Grammy and why.

Megan stopped in her tracks, suddenly aware of voices in the not-too-far distance. She felt like a trapped deer, unsure which direction to bolt. The voices didn't seem to get any louder or softer, so Megan assumed the people where stationary. She slowly and silently crept closer, wanting to see who it was and to possibly hear what they were saying. Cautiously, she lowered her body and began slithering toward the voices using the undergrowth as cover. After traveling a short distance, she spied them. It was Jake and Ethel.

"I don't care. I'll not get tangled in a mess by spyin' on someone for that … that woman!" Jake's face was red with anger as he spit the words out and stammered for a name to use.

"She wasn't askin' ya to spy on anyone. She just wants ya to keep your ears and eyes open, honey," Ethel patted Jake's chest as she spoke.

"'Pears to me like one thing leads to another where Carol's concerned, and I don't trust her any farther than I can throw a steer. I just know she had some part in the old lady's dyin'! I'm tellin' ya: I don't like it, and I won't have no part of it, and that's final! Are ya understandin' me, Ethel?"

"All right, Jake. I'll see if I can smooth things over with her and at least save your job," Ethel sulked down the path talking to herself under her breath.

Jake jerked his cap off and slung it to the ground mumbling profanities as he bent to retrieve it. He grabbed his pruners, which were leaning against a tree, and stomped away in the same direction Ethel had gone.

Megan rolled on her back gazing up at the trees and began trying to make sense out of the morning's events. Who did Carol want Jake to spy on and why? And what had Carol done in the past that was so wrong in Jake's eyes? Would Jake talk to her about Grammy's death and tell her what part he thought Carol played? Megan seemed to be getting more questions and no answers.

"What have I, correction, Mother, gotten me into?" she wondered as she glanced at her watch.
"Oh, my ... where did the morning go? I better hurry if I don't want to be late for lunch!"

Megan darted down the path toward the house. Jake looked startled as she bounded out of the woods past him. She flashed him her friendliest smile, waved, and continued down the path. When she reached the house, she went directly to the dining room without even washing her hands or face. No one was there and the table had not been set. As she headed to the kitchen, she looked at her watch again. According to it, she was right on schedule. She held her wrist to her ear to make sure her watch was running, and, as she heard the faint tick, she sighed in relief. When she entered the kitchen, Agnes began spooning food onto a plate. The kitchen table had been set for one, complete with freshly cut flowers from the garden.

"Miss Carol isn't home yet, and I thought you might enjoy eatin' in here for a change," Agnes said, almost more like a question than a statement.

"Oh, yes. Thank you so much," Megan conveyed her pleasure to the cook.

Agnes smiled her huge toothless grin and set Megan's plate on the table.

"Let me just run upstairs and wash my hands and face."

"There's a sink right there by that door, and I'll getcha a fresh towel if ya'd just as soon."

"You think of everything, Agnes. How would I ever get along without you?"

Agnes blushed at this comment and abruptly turned to a closet and brought out a clean, fluffy towel.

When Megan returned to the table, Agnes was nowhere in sight. Megan sighed in disappointment. She had hoped she and Agnes could visit while she ate. She loved listening to the tales Agnes told about when Grammy was alive. Megan was sure Grammy had not treated Agnes poorly like Carol did.

"I don't think I like my aunt very much," Megan concluded to herself. She finished her lunch, set her dishes in the sink, and returned to the patio.

She decided to have one more look around the outside of the house before tackling the inside. As she rounded the corner to the side of the house, the ground suddenly began sinking under her feet. As the earth began swallowing her, she desperately searched for something to grab hold of. All she could find was grass, and it came out by the roots as she descended deeper into the ground. Suddenly her head was underground and blocking the sun.

"I will not faint!" Megan said as her pulse quickened with her fright.

Chapter Four

Megan's feet hit something metal and immediately she landed rather clumsily on a cement floor. She sat on the cool floor letting her eyes adjust to the light and her mind analyze what had just happened. Slowly she looked at her surroundings.

"I'm in the basement!" she exclaimed out loud in her bewilderment. "I found the old coal chute, and, I don't know about dangerous, but it's certainly scary!" she chuckled to herself. "I can hardly wait to tell Troy!"

She began searching for signs of foul play and of flooding. She noticed every wall had a water stain midway up. When she came to the far corner, the floor was damp. As she looked up, she saw water dripping from an overhead pipe. Old pipes were stacked against the wall, and she realized the basement must've been flooded by broken water pipes.

"Why board up the basement, though? Why not just fix the pipes, which it appears someone did?"

One mystery was solved but with it came another one. Maybe Troy could help her figure it out on Friday when he came back. There was no indication of anything out of the ordinary, so Megan began searching for a way out of the basement. The stairs led to a wall and looked rather rotten, and she knew there was a heavy cupboard on the other side. She could never budge that even if the stairs could hold her weight and she could break through the wall! It appeared as though she would have to emerge the same way she had descended. As she began climbing up the chute, she could almost hear Grampy's scolding voice, but she knew it was her only way out of the basement.

As she heaved her body out of the chute and onto the grassy lawn, she noticed a metal cover leaning against the house. Upon examination she discovered it was a perfect fit over the opening to the coal chute.

"Someone moved it, hoping I would fall in and probably be critically injured!" she said horrified. "Who could have done that and why?"

Megan was visibly shaken now and covered from head to toe in soot. She returned the cover to its rightful place and slowly turned toward the house. In the distance she could see Jake standing by the trees and looking at her. She put her hands on her hips, stood with her legs slightly apart, and stared back. Her fear had been replaced with anger! Jake immediately appeared busy pruning trees.

"I haven't even met that man. Why would he do such a thing to me? Did he do such a thing? Gee whiz, I'm really confused now. Maybe I should return home while I have a little sanity left."

Megan felt she couldn't wait till Friday to talk things over with Troy. She felt real danger all around her. Just as she had done earlier, she quietly slipped into the woods and headed toward the tree with the hiding place. She needed to leave Troy a note telling him she needed to see him immediately. To her relief, as she put her hand into the tree, she felt a notepad and a pencil.

"Troy thinks of everything," she thought. She quickly scribbled her message, returned it and the pad and pencil to the hiding place, and retraced her steps back to the house.

Megan slipped into the house and arrived at her suite without being detected by anyone else. She removed her blackened clothes and stepped into the shower. Just as it had the first evening, the lavender-smelling foam calmed and relaxed her. When she had finally washed the soot off and gotten it all out of her tangled curls, she felt completely exhausted. She decided to lie down for a quick nap before snooping around the house.

Someone pounding on her door startled Megan awake.

"Who's there?" she inquired.

"It's Carol, and Troy's downstairs. Says he promised to take you out on the town tonight," Carol said through the closed door.

"Oh, yes. Tell him I'm running a bit late but will be down shortly, please. And, Carol … thank you."

As Megan tried to sit up, she felt like she had been run over by a truck. Every muscle in her body ached. She dressed, applied makeup, brushed her hair as quickly as her sore body would allow, and headed for the stairs. She knew there'd be no sliding down the banister tonight!

Troy, grinning from ear to ear, met her at the bottom of the stairs with a quick peck on her cheek. She played along since Carol seemed to be watching their every move.

"Is there any certain time I should be back?" Megan inquired of Carol.

"Certainly not!" Carol retorted. "Why would you even ask such a question? This is a guest ranch not a college dorm!"

"Well, I seem to have broken so many rules today I didn't want to upset you by breaking another one," Megan replied using her most innocent voice.

With that, Carol turned and marched toward the kitchen grumbling under her breath.

"What was that all about?" Troy whispered as they headed for the door.

"I've got much to tell you when we are alone with no prying eyes or ears," she promised.

Troy held her car door open for her and couldn't help noticing her frown as she sat down and swung her legs into the car.

"Are you all right?" he asked unable to hide his concern. "You look as if you're in pain!"

"I am, and that's one of the things I'll tell you about later," she replied honestly. "What are your plans for tonight, anyway? I didn't expect you to respond to my note so quickly!"

"What note? I found out some facts today that I thought you should know as soon as possible."

"I left a note in the tree saying I needed to talk to you as soon as possible. It sounds as though we both had a productive day, but you didn't answer my question regarding your plans."

"Oh, yeah. Well, I really didn't make any plans. I just thought I'd take ya out for a bite to eat, and you can plan the rest of the evenin'. How's that sound to ya?"

"That sounds great. Is there somewhere quiet we could talk without being overheard?"

"There's always my little ol' place," he grinned mischievously at her.

Megan laughed out loud and had to grab her sore ribs. "Do you promise to behave if we go there after we eat?" she asked seriously.

"I suppose," Troy answered trying to sound dejected and putting a pout on his face. "Now, tell me why you're so sore," he insisted.

Megan related the events of her day leaving nothing out. Troy pulled the car into a slot in front of the only diner in town just as she finished. He cut the engine, leaned across the seat, and held her face in his hands. Then he did the unexpected. He kissed her. Not a peck on the forehead like she was expecting, but a lingering kiss on her lips.
"I don't know what I'd do if anythin' happened to you. You must promise me that you'll be on your guard from now on," he was almost whispering.

He immediately turned and got out of the car without giving Megan a chance to respond. He walked around the car, helped her out of the car, and led her inside the diner as though nothing at all had happened.
"How in the world does he do that?" she wondered. She was still a bit breathless and felt dazed.

As they selected a table, they noticed Viola and Ethel sitting in a booth at the back of the diner. Ethel's back was toward them, but they both waved to Viola. She suddenly looked away without acknowledging them at all.

"How strange," Megan commented.

There was that lopsided grin that Megan knew meant trouble. "She's probably feelin' jilted since I'm here with you," Troy said smugly.

"Nothing's ever your fault, is it? Fine, I'll take the blame this time, I guess," she responded jokingly.

As they continued this playful banter and ordered their meals, Viola left her table headed for the restroom. When she emerged, she waved at them as though it were the first time she'd seen them that evening. As she approached their table, Troy rose to his feet. Viola went straight to him and began patting and rubbing his chest while she flirted and batted her eyes at him. Finally she turned toward Megan, nodded her head, and walked back to her booth. She and Ethel soon left without either looking in Megan and Troy's direction.

"What a strange old lady she has become," Megan commented. "I don't remember her being like that at all when I used to visit. Sometimes she and Grammy acted and sounded just alike. They both used to call me 'Angel,' and, if I didn't see which one of them said it, I wasn't sure which one to look at when I answered," she continued with a giggle.

"I remember that," Troy said. "She changed after Grammy died. They were as close as two sisters, if not closer, and, unfortunately, she was the one who was stayin' with Grammy the night she died, yanno."

"Yes, I know," sighed Megan. "I wish there were something I could do to make her feel better."

When they had finished their meal, they stepped out into the cool Texas evening. As the door to the diner closed, Troy took Megan's hand in his. She smiled up at him and made no attempt to pull away from his touch. Somehow it felt natural to her. After moving around some, Megan didn't feel as sore and stiff as she had when she first woke from her nap. Troy noticed that her disposition seemed to be a bit lighter, and he was happy.

"Still wanna go to my place and compare notes?" he asked after they were settled back in the car.

"Yes, I think that would be our best bet," she answered without hesitation.

"I have somethin' I wanna show ya there, anyway. Like a nincompoop, I forgot to bring it with me!" he informed her.

"Oh? What is it?" she demanded, never wanting to wait for anything.

"You'll just hafta wait and see, missy," he said in the sternest voice he could muster. "It's somethin' I got from a friend at the hospital today."

"Another admirer, I suppose," she teased him.

"Yeah, I guess ya could say that. Her name's Jane Miller, and she's been head nurse at the hospital for quite some time. Maybe you can meet her one of these days."

"Perhaps I can," Megan smiled at him. She didn't relish meeting another woman who was interested in Troy.

Troy turned off the main road onto a tree-lined gravel road when they reached the outskirts of town. The road ended in a circle drive in front of a massive stone and glass house. Megan had never seen anything so beautiful.

The lawn was immaculate, and the flowerbeds were all abloom. Spotlights shone on the flowerbeds and the house seemed to sparkle like the sequins on a singer's dress when she walks on stage.

"Who lives here?" Megan asked breathlessly.

Troy looked pleased by her reaction as he told her, "I do."

"This is your 'little ol' place'?" she asked unbelievingly.

"Well, yeah. Ya see, I kinda like to build. Dad thinks I got carried away a bit; but one thing seemed to call for another, and you're lookin' at the finished product," Troy had to fight back the laughter and his pride at her expression.

He got out and went to help her out. Megan wasn't sure she could even move she was so shocked. Troy patiently stood by her door with his right hand extended until she finally sighed, took his hand, and stepped out of the car. He thought the soreness and stiffness had returned with her sitting in the car. He immediately slipped his left arm around her waist to help support her, and they headed for the front door. The cool air seemed to help her regain her senses, and she was feeling almost normal by the time they stepped onto the marble floor of the entry. Megan wanted to stand still and memorize every detail of the beautiful sight in front of her, but Troy was guiding her into another room.

Here he released her and asked, "May I get ya somethin' to drink while ya look around?"

"I'd love some iced tea, no sugar, but lemon if you have it."

"Comin' right up. Now don't be bashful; just make yerself right at home!" He winked at her as he turned and headed for the kitchen.

A beautiful fireplace with rock that matched the outside of the house completely occupied one wall in this room. The adjoining wall was solid glass and overlooked a lake. Megan settled into the soft cushions of the sofa that faced the fireplace, kicked her shoes off, and tucked one leg under her body.
"I could sit right here for the rest of my life!" she sighed to herself.

As Troy came in with their tea, she asked, "You really built this place yourself?"

"Yeah. Ya didn't know I was so talented, did ya? I studied architecture in college. I really thought that was what I wanted for my career. Dad was in a car accident and was hurt badly enough to cause his retirement soon after I graduated. Of course I immediately returned home to be of what help I could to 'im. I assisted 'im in closin' some cases he just couldn't bear to leave open, and I found the work quite interestin'. Yep, you guessed it; I made a career change."

With that he shrugged his shoulders and laughed.

"So you spent your spare time building this lovely home," she concluded for him. "I'll bet the view is spectacular during the winter. You have such pretty snows here. Everything looks so pristine and clean, unlike the dirty-looking slush the traffic causes in New York.

"I'm a bit curious, though," she continued as she stepped barefooted to the gigantic window. "Doesn't the cold air of winter and the hot air of summer come through such a huge window?"

"Touch it," he told her.

She was surprised that it felt tepid even though it was cool outside. "What gives?" she asked unable to contain her curiosity.

Troy joined her by the window and replied proudly, "It's a triple-paned window. The center pane is one I developed myself. It deflects heat and cold both. The patent is pendin', but, as soon as it's approved, I intend to start production. I figure I can create around five hundred jobs initially and even more if it's in demand like I think it will be."

"How wonderful for you and the town!" she said as she turned, patted his chest, and headed back to the sofa. "What's that?" she asked referring to a rustling noise from his shirt pocket.

"I dunno. Let me get my readin' glasses," he said as he fished a folded note from his pocket.

As he crossed from his desk back to the sofa, he read the note to himself not sure if it was something he'd want to share with Megan. When he'd finished reading it, he plopped down on the sofa almost bouncing Megan to the floor.

"I'm not sure what to make of this," he said with a puzzled frown. "This note is from Viola! She must've slipped it in my pocket when she was fussin' over me at the restaurant!"

"You're kidding! Are you going to tell me what it says, or are you going to keep me guessing all night?" Megan asked impatiently.

"I'm sorry. Of course I'm gonna read it to ya!" Troy quietly began to read: "Watch over our Angel closely! There are those who would cause her grave bodily harm if the opportunity arises! Her life is literally in your hands!"

It was signed "Viola."

"What? Does it really say 'Angel'?" Megan was as bewildered as Troy.

He handed her the note so she could see for herself.

"She knows who I am!" Megan practically shouted.

Chapter Five

Megan and Troy both fell silent letting their minds comprehend the contents of Viola's note. Both were utterly shocked by the revelations it held.

Finally Megan spoke, "How would she know who I am?" she asked accusingly.

"I dunno," Troy answered, putting emphasis on the "I". "You don't seriously think I would've told her or anyone else, do ya?" he asked, sounding truly hurt.

Megan looked into his eyes and knew he wouldn't have blown her cover.

"I'm sorry. Of course I know you wouldn't have told anyone. I guess I'm just tired and stressed," she said as she leaned forward clasping her hands together and stretching her back.

"Turn your back toward me, and I'll see if I can help your sore, tired muscles any," Troy commanded her.

Megan sat cross-legged like an Indian with her back to Troy. He gently massaged her shoulders and arms. Soon she felt her muscles relaxing.

"You better stop that or I'll fall asleep, and we have much business to take care of."

Megan turned and tucked one leg under her body. Troy went back to his desk, withdrew a key from his pocket, and opened a drawer. He withdrew two papers, locked the drawer back, and returned to the sofa and Megan's side. He handed one of the papers to her.

"This is Grammy's discharge paper from her stay in the hospital. Jane made me a copy today. Look at the diagnosis!"

Megan scanned the paper for the diagnosis.
"'Arsenic poisoning'?" she read aloud, unable to believe it.

"Yeah. Now look at the cause of death on this copy of the death certificate."

"'Possible arsenic poisoning by person or persons unknown!' That should've told them to perform an autopsy! And why isn't your office still investigating this?"

Megan could hold back the tears no longer. Doc believed someone had poisoned her Grammy! Why didn't he perform an autopsy? Did he suspect anyone? Who had anything to gain by Grammy's death? Carol! All these thoughts and questions filled Megan's head as she sobbed uncontrollably. Troy put his arm around her and she laid her head on his shoulder, but he couldn't think of any comforting words.

Megan felt like she had cried for an eternity, and the front of Troy's shirt was soaked. He pulled his shirt tail out and offered it to her to blow her nose. Now she was laughing uncontrollably! Troy just sat there, still holding her, and patiently waited for her to once again gain control of her emotions.

"He must think I'm a lunatic," she thought as she tried to stop laughing.

When she had settled down some, Troy went to change his shirt, and she went to the restroom to wash her face. They both returned to the living room at the same time.

"Quite a night, huh?" Troy smiled at her.

"That's an understatement if I've ever heard one. I wonder if Doc would answer a few questions for me?" she said as she once again sat on the sofa.

"How're ya gonna ask 'im without lettin' 'im know who ya are? I think Viola's our best bet."

"I wish I could have Grammy's body exhumed and an autopsy performed," Megan said more to herself than to Troy.

"You'd definitely hafta reveal your identity for that!"

"Do you think it would be dangerous for me to admit to everyone who I really am?"

"I don't think now is the time to do that. I wanna know who wants to harm you and why, first."

Just the thought of someone wanting to bring Megan harm made Troy angry. He intended to learn their identity as soon as possible.

Megan had been turning the events of the day and these new discoveries over in her mind. Some of the puzzle pieces seemed to be fitting together.

"I'm the person Carol wanted Jake to spy on!" she announced. "And I'll bet she's the one who wants to harm me. But why would she? As far as she knows, I'm just a guest at her ranch who wants to spend the summer with her boyfriend."

"That's why I wanna talk to Viola. She apparently knows who wants to harm you. Maybe she knows why, too. In the meantime, we need to stay in close contact with each other. I wanna know where you are and what you're doin' at all times. I know that sounds like I'm a control freak, but I just wanna be able to protect you as much as possible. Do ya understand? "

Megan patted his chest and assured him she understood. It made her feel special instead of resentful.
"I need to examine these feelings more closely when I'm alone," she told herself.

"Are you going to try to see Viola tomorrow, then?"

"Yeah, I think so. I'm also gonna ask the sheriff about the investigation into Grammy's death. He wouldn't have assigned the case to me 'cause I was too close to Grammy but I wanna know who's in charge of the investigation and what's happenin'."

"Do you think it would raise any eyebrows if I went to the cemetery? I'd like to see Grammy's grave and pay my respects since I was unable to attend the funeral."

"Take your camera with ya, and, if anyone shows up lookin' curious, tell 'em ya collect pictures of old tombstones. There's some out there datin' back to the seventeen hundreds."

"What a great idea! Are you always so good at lying?"

"Uh, I stand on the fifth."

"Well, then, I guess I'm going to have to question anything you say to me from now on." Megan loved the playful banter they always seemed to get into. It helped relax her.

"I'd never lie to you, Megan!" Troy said suddenly serious.

Megan wasn't sure how to reply, so she just smiled at him and patted his chest. He took her hand before she could remove it from his chest, and gently turned it over, and kissed her palm. This time the heat didn't start up her neck. She leaned into him and kissed that crooked grin. She admitted to herself at that very instant that she was falling for this country bumpkin! They sat for a while just holding each other and savoring the moment.

Megan sat up, to Troy's disappointment, and looked at her watch.

"It's really late, Troy. You had best take me back to the ranch now."

"Okay, if you insist," Troy couldn't help showing his disappointment.

The trip back to the ranch was spent in a peaceful silence with Megan sitting in the middle of the seat close to Troy. As they turned off the highway onto the graveled road leading to the ranch, Troy broke the silence.

"Yanno, I have a bunch of vacation time built up. I think I'll ask to take it now, and we can investigate together. The sheriff can't say nuttin' 'bout me nosin' into Grammy's death if I'm doin' it on my own time. Then I wouldn't hafta worry about you. I could be with ya all the time."

"You're so sweet. If you're sure that's what you want to do, it sounds great to me. I know I'd feel a lot safer knowing you had my back."

"Okay, it's settled then. Now don't forget to call me on my cell phone tomorrow if you go anywhere besides the cemetery."

"Yes, dear. I won't forget," Megan teased him.

Troy walked Megan to the door, kissed her good night, and returned to his car as she went inside. When he saw the light in her suite come on, he started the engine and headed down the graveled road.

Megan' smiling the whole time, watched from her window until the taillights of Troy's car disappeared.

"He really does care about me," she sighed. She glanced at the time as she laid her watch on the nightstand. "Too late to call Mom tonight," she scolded herself. She had only called once since her arrival and knew May would be wondering what she had discovered. "I'll call first thing in the morning!" she promised.

Megan slept soundly all night and awoke refreshed. She immediately grabbed her cell phone and stepped out onto the balcony. After checking for anyone who was within earshot, she dialed May's number. Megan had no intention of telling her mother about Viola saying she was in danger, but she did want to tell her about Viola knowing who she was. She also wanted to suggest May come to the ranch and ask for an autopsy on Grammy's body. Then Megan wouldn't have to blow her cover. Someone finally answered the phone at May's, and Megan immediately recognized the voice of the housekeeper.

"Alice?"

Megan panicked. Had May been hospitalized? Before she could ask, the housekeeper informed her May had gone to brunch with an old friend who was in town. Megan was relieved to learn that May was feeling well enough to go somewhere but was disappointed she had missed her.

"Could you give her a message when she returns?"

"Of course. I'd be most happy to."

"Tell her I called and all is fine. I'll try to call again this evening."

"Oh, yes, I'll be sure and tell her. She was somewhat concerned about you before she left. Don't worry, I'll tell her, and I'm glad you're all right!"

Megan thanked the housekeeper and returned to her room. She quickly showered, dressed, and put on makeup. She grabbed her watch and camera before leaving her rooms. As she entered the dining room, Carol was just sitting down to eat breakfast.

"Good morning," Carol said with a smile. "I'm glad you could join me for breakfast this morning. I don't like eating alone, do you?"

"Good morning," Megan returned Carol's smile. "I've grown accustom to eating alone, I guess."

"Well, you won't have to this morning!" Carol eagerly said. Carol made Megan feel uneasy when she was this friendly. She wondered what Carol was up to.

"*She probably poisoned the food after fixing her plate!*" she thought. Megan opted for just a cup of coffee and some juice.

"I'm going to the cemetery to take some pictures of old tombstones to add to my collection. I'm not sure how much walking that will entail, so I best not eat much," she explained as she sat down next to Carol.

"Oh, there's some really old, pretty ones toward the back of the cemetery," Carol offered.

"Yes, Troy, was telling me about them last night."

"Did you two have fun last night? Ethel told me you were at the diner."
"Yes, we were, and, yes, we did. When did you talk to Ethel?"

"Oh, she calls me every morning to see if I need any help," Carol explained. "She really is a dear friend. I don't know how I would have made it without her after Mama passed away."

"I don't mean to be nosy or to upset you," Megan began, "but was your mother ill?"

"Oh, no. She was as healthy as a horse! She ... she fell down the stairs," Carol stammered and wiped a tear off her check as she spoke.

"How awful for you!" Megan patted Carol's hand, and Carol grasped Megan's as though she could gain some strength from her.

"Losing my Mama was the worst thing I've ever gone through!" Tears were now flowing down Carol's face, and she didn't even attempt to catch them. "I have no idea where my sister is, so Ethel is the only one I had to comfort me and help with the arrangements. Viola was so upset that she spent three days locked in her room refusing to talk to anyone!"

"Why don't you know where your sister is?" Megan was determined to get Carol's viewpoint while she was in a talkative mood.

Carol wiped her eyes and blew her nose on her napkin. Megan feared their conversation was over, but Carol looked at her and attempted a smile.
"I was a rather stupid teenager," she began, "and I left my country home bound for New York when I was only sixteen. I had no doubt that I would bowl the city over with my beauty and everyone would want me to model for their agency! I guess I should've said I was very stupid!
"Needless to say, I almost starved to death and was among the homeless in New York. My parents would've welcomed me with open arms, but my pride wouldn't let me call them. By chance I asked a social worker, whose name was Beth, for a handout one day. She took me to a nearby diner and bought me some food. She asked nothing from me and left when I finished eating.

"She came back two or three times a week and took me to lunch. We talked and got to know each other quite well. One day when I finished eating, Beth offered me a way off of the streets. She needed someone to stay with her mother while she was at work. She would give me room and board and send me to night school for my services.

"That was the turning point of my life! I got an education and became the manager of a hotel in New York. Beth's mother rented a suite in the hotel, and the entire staff and I watched over her until the day she died. She was the closest thing to a mother that I'd had for a long time!"

Megan did not rush Carol as she sat remembering the impact this lady had on her life.

Finally Carol sighed and continued, "Beth encouraged me to call my parents. I did, and they wanted me to come home, at least for a visit. I really had missed them and my sister, so I took a few days off and flew home. I had a wonderful visit with my parents, but my sister, May, had married and moved away. The last time I saw her was at Papa's funeral. She had a little girl, but she left her with her husband, so I've never seen her. May's husband had to move quite often because of his job, and over the years we lost touch with each other."

"That's too bad," Megan said sincerely. "Perhaps one day your paths will cross again," she added as she squeezed Carol's hand and stood. "Will you be all right if I leave? I don't want to lose the morning light for my photos."

"Sure," Carol assured her. "Thank you for listening to my woeful tale."

"I was glad you shared it with me. Maybe we can talk again, and I can tell you my woeful tale," Megan giggled.

Megan felt much closer to her aunt as she started her car and headed for the cemetery. She could hardly wait to talk to May that evening and tell her about her talk with Carol.

Troy had told Megan where Grammy's gravesite was, but she drove past it when she entered the cemetery. She did not want to park her car by it just in case someone else appeared and was curious. Instead she drove to the back of the cemetery where Carol had told her some of the older tombstones were. She would park there, take some pictures, and work her way toward Grammy's grave. She parked, grabbed her camera and keys, and started reading tombstones. She was just about to snap a picture when she heard the loud crack of wood breaking and then her head hit the hard base of the tombstone as she was knocked unconscious.

Chapter Six

Troy had spent most of the morning at the sheriff's office where he learned the sheriff was personally investigating Grammy's death. So far, what few leads he had, turned up nothing. By all appearances, her death resulted from a fall down the stairs. The only evidence pointing to homicide was the death certificate, and the doctor was determined he was right. The sheriff was ready to conclude accidental death and file the case as a cold case. He felt the doctor was convinced she had been poisoned because of her hospital stay the month before, but he knew some other folks in the county that had been poisoned by arsenic in their water well. They had their wells treated and all was fine. Troy was determined to find out if Grammy's well had been tested for arsenic. If not, he intended to pay for it to be tested himself.

While at the office, Troy asked to take his vacation days effective immediately. The sheriff said that would be fine and told the secretary to see how many days Troy had accumulated. Troy felt excited as he left the office knowing he would not return for three weeks. He whistled a happy tune as he hurried to his car thinking about spending three weeks with Megan. He wondered if he ought to call her and tell her the good news but decided it would be best to wait until he had talked with Viola. He was supposed to meet Viola at the library in ten minutes.

Troy found Viola at the computers. He didn't realize the old lady even knew how to type, let alone run a computer.

"Whatcha doin' there, beautiful?" he flirted as he sat down next to her.

"Oh, I have a friend in Florida, and I come here to chat with her. Ethel doesn't like for me to run the phone bill up, yanno," she smiled at him.

"I didn't know you knew anyone in Florida. What's her or his name?"

"Why, Troy, if I didn't know better, I'd think you were jealous!" she teased. "Not that it's any of yer business, but her name is Edith Guthrie."

"Is she from these parts? I don't believe I know her."

"No, you wouldn't know her. She moved away while we were still in school. You weren't even a twinkle in yer daddy's eye yet," she winked at him. "What did you want to see me about?" she asked after she had said good-bye to Edith.

"The note you put in my pocket." Troy was very serious now and there was a burrow between his brows.

"That's what I figured. This is not a very private place, though, and I'd rather no one heard this conversation, if ya know what I mean."

"Yes, I agree." Troy was silent, thinking for a while, and then he said, "How about my place? I'll leave first and you follow in ten minutes."

"Gotcha," she said as she gave him a thumbs-up.

Troy was grinning as he left the library and got into his car.
"What a silly old woman. She acted just like she was a spy or sumthin'. I want to check on this Edith Guthrie, too. Sumthin' just doesn't seem right about her," he thought.

He left his car in the circle drive, entered the house, and made a pot of coffee. Exactly ten minutes later, Viola pulled into the drive and parked directly behind him. She was glad trees and shrubbery blocked the drive from the view of motorists just passing by. She knew there would be questions to answer if anyone discovered her at Troy's house. She was still standing beside her car gazing toward the road when Troy opened the front door.

"Come on in here, beautiful!" he shouted to her.

Viola turned and walked toward him. "Don't start none of yer flirtin' with me!" she scolded.

"My flirtin'? Seems to me you are the flirt around here."

"Well, now's not the time or place," she said as she stepped into the house.

Troy led her to the kitchen table, poured coffee for them both, and sat down beside her. They both sipped their coffee waiting for the other to speak. Troy knew Viola could be quite stubborn when she took the notion, so he broke the silence.

"How did you know who Megan is?" "Lands sake, boy, I'm not brain-dead! She has the same smile and the same twinkle in her eye that she had as a child. Plus now she acts and moves a bit like Edna did." Viola's voice broke and tears started to form as she spoke Grammy's name.

"Well, we both think you're mighty smart to have figured it out so soon!" he complimented. "I guess you've also discerned that she's here to find out more about Grammy's death."

"Yep, I figured that, and I sure hope she can figure out more than the cops have!" she almost spat the words at him. "I wish I could help her, but I'm afraid I don't know much. I know someone had poisoned her the month before, but I don't know who or why."

"I'm sure a smart lady like you has an idea or two, though," Troy said encouraging her to confide in him.

"Well, sure, I do, but I'd not wanna tell without proof. That wouldn't be right, now would it?"

"No, I guess not," Troy couldn't hide the disappointment in his voice or his face.
Viola felt bad and was debating whether or not to confide her thoughts in him when he changed the subject.

"In your note, you said Megan was in danger. Who would want to harm her and why?" he asked resting his elbows on the table.

"I don't know that either," Viola shook her head and continued. "I overheard Ethel talkin' to someone on the phone. She nevah pays any attention to me. Thinks I'm senile and that no one would believe me even if I knew what was goin' on. Anyways, I heard her say that they were goin' to hafta do sumthin' about that nosy parker, Megan. No one other than me knows who she is or why she's here, but she's been seen nosin' around the house and grounds."

"So you think your daughter-in-law means to harm Megan?" Troy couldn't believe what he was hearing.

"I don't wanna think that, but what else am I to think? By the way, where is Megan and why aren't you with her?"

"She went to the cemetery to get some pictures of some of the old tombstones for her collection." Troy's answer alarmed Viola.
"Who knew she was goin' there?" she asked.

"Just me, I reckon. As far as I know, she didn't tell anyone else."

"Did ya ever think maybe someone could've followed her?" Viola was already up and heading for the door. "You do as ya please, but I'm headin' for the cemetery. And you best pray that Angel child hasn't been harmed while we sat jackin' our jaws!"

Troy grabbed his keys and sped out of the driveway, throwing gravel at everything behind him, before Viola had her car started.
"*Reckless youngin!*" Viola thought as the gravel pelted her car and windshield.

The short trip to the cemetery seemed to take hours since Troy was so anxious. As he turned into the gate, he spotted Megan's car parked on the back road in the oldest part of the cemetery. He quickly scanned the surrounding area but saw no sign of Megan. He steered his car toward hers and came to a screeching halt as he saw Megan on the ground with her head in a pool of blood. He grabbed his police radio and called dispatch requesting an ambulance immediately. As he was talking to the dispatcher, he reached under the seat and retrieved his first aid kit. He was already stepping out of his car as he signed off the radio. He had just knelt beside Megan's unconscious body when Viola arrived.

Troy immediately began assessing Megan's injuries. There was dried blood and a huge bump on the back of her head, but the worst injury seemed to be on the front of her head. He removed gauze squares from the kit and tried to apply pressure to the gaping wound without moving her.
Viola looked as though she were about to faint, so he told her to go back to her car and wave the ambulance toward them when she saw it. She was glad to get some distance between her and the blood.

The EMT stabilized Megan and put her in the ambulance. As they left the cemetery, sirens blaring, Viola followed, determined not to let Megan out of her sight again. Left alone, Troy began looking for clues. He grabbed his crime scene kit from the trunk of his car and began photographing and bagging evidence. There wasn't much evidence there: a broken board with blood and some of Megan's red curls on one end and Megan's camera, which he wasn't sure would be considered evidence. He bagged it anyway and had just finished when the sheriff arrived.

"I thought I put you on vacation time this mornin', Troy. Whatcha got?" the sheriff asked.

"My friend was already knocked unconscious when I got here," Troy explained. "I've bagged what little evidence there is, including the camera Megan was using to take pictures of the tombstones."

Troy handed the bags to the sheriff.
"I'll head for the hospital in Amarillo if ya don't have any more questions for me."

"No, not now. I'll need to talk to the girl as soon as possible, though. Which hospital is she in?"
The two men walked toward Troy's car together as they talked.

"High Plains," Troy told him, "and that's where I'll be if ya need me for anything."

As Troy headed for the gate to the cemetery, he looked in his rearview mirror and saw the sheriff standing by the grave scratching his head. He let out a sigh and began praying for Megan as the tears rolled down his cheek.

When Troy arrived at the hospital, he found Viola waiting in the front lobby for him. All of a sudden, he realized just how old she was. She looked so haggard that he couldn't resist putting his arm around her and pulling her close to him on the bench. She seemed so fragile.

"She's still in the ER," Viola reported. "They don't think her injuries are too serious, but she does have a concussion and requires stitches. They want to keep her for a few days."

"I figured they would," Troy patted Viola's shoulder trying to comfort her. "You were right, Viola; I should've been with her. I'll never forgive myself for not listenin' to ya!"

"There's no time for either of us to take a guilt trip!" Viola scolded. "We've gotta find the person who hurt our Angel before they get a chance to hurt her worse!"

"Yes, of course. You are right as rain. I guess I oughtta call her mother and let her know what's happened, too." Troy said.

"May? You know how to contact May? "Viola asked amazed.

"Yes, it was her idea for Megan to come do some snoopin'. She never thought Megan was in any danger."

"Well, I nevah," Viola was so surprised by this news she could think of nothing to say.

The doctor approached them and told them the same news Viola had just related to Troy. He gave them her room number but told them to limit their visits until further notice because she was going to need her rest. He gave Troy permission to stay with her as long as he didn't interfere with her care in any way.

After the doctor left, Viola headed for Megan's room, and Troy headed outside to call May. He was not looking forward to telling her, so he decided to call his dad instead. Roy had gone to New York and was planning on visiting May while there. Troy was hoping to persuade Roy to tell her the news of Megan.

Roy was delighted to hear his son's voice, and Troy was delighted to hear that Roy was at May's apartment.

"Dad, there's been … huh … well … an incident here," Troy began.

"What kinda incident?" Roy sometimes became impatient with his son's way of stumbling over words. "Just gimme the facts as concisely as possible."

"Megan was attacked and is in the hospital. Is that concise enough for ya?" Troy was not in the mood for his father's impatience!

"How bad?" was all Roy said.

"Concussion and fifteen stitches in her head above the right temple. Also contusion to the back of the head from blunt force. Somebody broke a two-by-four on the back of her head, Dad!"

"Any idea who?"

"Not yet."

"I'll call ya back. I need to explain all this to May and talk our options over with her."

"Okay. 'Bout how long do ya think before ya call? I haven't seen Megan since they sewed her up, and I don't wanna make her think I don't care."

"That sounds like a whole 'nother story, but we'll discuss that later. Gimme an hour."

Roy could tell his son was worried and truly cared about Megan by his tone of voice. He couldn't help but smile because he was beginning to have feelings for May, too.

Troy hung up his cell phone and hurried into the hospital to see Megan.

He met Viola as she was leaving. She said Megan was still sleeping, so she was going to go home. She didn't want to raise any suspicions where Ethel was concerned. She promised to keep her eyes and ears open and her mouth shut.

Troy sat in the chair by Megan's bed, holding her hand and watching her sleep for almost an hour. As he left to go outside and wait for his dad's call, he told the nurse where he'd be and instructed her to send someone to get him if there were any change before he returned.

He had just stepped through the automatic door when his phone began ringing.

"May and I are headin' for the airport now," Roy boomed. "We arrive in Amarillo at seven-thirty this evenin'. Pick us up. We're on United flight 185."

"You sound like a talkin' telegram!" Troy laughed.

"Sorry. This really caught us by surprise. We didn't feel Megan would be in any danger," Roy explained.

"Yeah, well, just wait till ya hear what we've discovered since she's been here. Is May gonna let everyone know who she is and that Megan is her daughter?"

"I think so. We're gonna discuss that more on the flight, and she'd like your input, too."

"Okay. I'm eager to meet her again. I'll bring yawl up to date on information when I pick ya up at seven-thirty. I'll even take yawl out to eat!"

"Wow. I'm impressed. Wait. 'You'll take us.' Does that mean you'll be drivin' us, but I hafta pay?" Roy teased.

"You catch on fast for an old man!" Troy returned.

They both laughed and hung up. Troy quickly called Carol so she wouldn't be wondering what had happened to her guest and then returned to the hospital and Megan's side to wait for their parents to arrive.

Chapter Seven

The first thing Megan saw when she awoke was Troy. He was holding her hand in both of his and leaning toward the bed with his head bowed.

She tried to speak, but her throat was so dry nothing came out but a gurgling sound. Troy's head immediately whipped up, and she saw terror in his eyes. She smiled to reassure him and mouthed the word "water." Troy looked relieved and poured some cool water into a glass. He held the glass and put the straw to her lips so she could drink.

"Thank you," she said when her throat finally got moist. "What happened to me?"

Troy sat on the side of her bed and held her hand again. "Someone hitcha on the back of the head with a two-by-four. You fell forward and hit the base of a tombstone. You have a concussion and some stitches." He gently stroked the left side of her forehead with his other hand as he talked. "Your mother is on her way. Her flight arrives at seven-thirty, and I'll hafta leave ya to go pick 'em up."

"You called my mother? Why?" Megan sounded upset.

"I thought she'd wanna know, and I thought you'd want her to know," Troy replied defensively.

"Them? Who else is coming?"

"My dad was up there visitin' your mom. Why are ya so upset with me?" Megan's attitude had Troy confused.

"I'm sorry. I'm not really upset with you. I'm upset that I let this happen. I should've had my guard up after Viola's warning. Is Mom all right? She has a bad heart, you know."

"Yeah, she's just fine. I think she's tougher than you give her credit for bein'," Troy was beginning to relax again. He didn't like it when Megan sounded mad.

"I'm gonna take 'em out to eat after I pick 'em up, and bring 'em up to date on what we've found out."

"Oh, that will be good. Wish I could go, too." Megan squeezed his hand as though it were in his power to release her from the hospital.

"Well, you're stuck right here for a day or so, I'm afraid. While I'm gone, you can take a nap so you'll be rested and feel like talkin' when we get back," he kissed her cheek as though he was tucking a child into bed for the night.

"I will if you'll give me a real kiss," she bribed him.

In spite of the fact that Megan was injured, Troy felt as if he were walking on clouds as he left the hospital. He wanted to whistle a merry tune and skip, but he bridled his enthusiasm.

Troy was relieved to see the plane was on schedule when he checked the board at the airport. He didn't want to leave Megan alone any longer than necessary. Roy and May were among the first people to leave the plane. After securing their luggage, they headed for Troy's car. As they walked, Troy reported on Megan's progress assuring May that Megan would probably be released the next day.

"I want to take her home immediately, but I know my daughter, so I came prepared to stay awhile," May told Troy.

"That was wise," Troy grinned at her. "No way will Megan leave until she knows what's goin' on, and who co-cocked her. She has some other things she wants to discuss with you, too, May."

"Tonight?" May asked incredulously. "Shouldn't she be resting?"

"Yes, she should, but you know Megan. She's just like a bulldog when she gets her teeth into somethin'."

May laughed for the first time since she heard Megan had been injured. "I see you have already got to know Megan very well."

Troy took Roy and May to Western Sizzlin' to eat. "The booths here are fairly private so we can talk," he explained.

After they had ordered their steaks and helped themselves to the salad bar, they settled into their booth. Troy brought them up to date on what had been happening and what they had discovered.

"Do you honestly expect me to believe that someone was poisoning my mother?" May asked when Troy had finished.

Troy tapped the death certificate that he had laid on the table, "That's what Doc put on this."

"Why wasn't there an autopsy?"

"No one ordered one. Unless a family member orders an autopsy, one is not performed in the state of Texas."

"Is it too late to have one done now?"

Troy chuckled, "You sound just like your daughter. I think that's one of the things she wants to talk to you about."

"In answer to your question," Roy interjected, "a family member would have to sign forms requesting the body be exhumed and an autopsy be performed."

"Part of me thinks we should just let Mama rest in peace, but the other part thinks we should do everything in our power to find out why she was taken from us. I talked to her on the phone the night before she supposedly fell down the stairs. She sounded great and assured me she was feeling well."

"You don't have to make a decision tonight, yanno. Think it over and discuss it with Megan," Roy said patting her hand.

May smiled warmly at him, "I don't know how I would have made it through this without you. I draw so much strength from you!"

At this show of affection, Troy excused himself and went to pay the cashier. It seemed strange to see a woman make over his dad in such a manner. He wasn't sure if he liked it or not. It had been just Troy and his dad since he could remember, and he wasn't sure he wanted to share Roy with a stranger. Sure, he had known May when he was a kid; but that had been a lifetime ago, and she was a stranger now. Roy and May joined Troy at the cashier's stand just as he finished paying the bill. They returned to the car and drove to the hospital in silence, each deep in their own thoughts.

As they entered her room, Megan and May both started talking at the same time. Troy and Roy just looked at each other as the women continued conversing in this manner. Neither woman was ever silent, but each managed to answer the other's questions. Both men thought it was quite interesting to observe. Finally Troy suggested he take his dad to get his car, so the men left, the women to themselves.

"Mom, I need to discuss something with you," Megan said after the men had left.

"Okay, but first, I want to know how you'd feel if I had Grammy's body exhumed and an autopsy performed."

Megan burst into laughter, scaring her mother. May saw nothing funny about what she had just said and decided Megan must be delirious from the head wounds. Just as May reached for the button to call a nurse to assist her daughter, Megan gained control over her laughter.

"That's exactly what I was going to discuss with you! Like mother, like daughter?"

"I don't know about that, but you scared me to death, young lady!" May teasingly scolded her daughter.

"I'm sorry, Mom, but surely you see the humor now."

May smiled at Megan, "Yes, I suppose I do, but I don't find it as hilarious as you did."

"That's because you're not on the drugs I'm on," Megan explained raising her eyebrows.

"That's not funny at all! You best quit with the comedian routine before someone throws tomatoes at you!"

"Okay, I'll be serious. I would like an autopsy performed. It's only fair to Grammy that we find out why she really died!"

"Yes, I agree, honey," May replied as she patted Megan's arm. "I'll talk to the officials tomorrow and see how soon it can be done."

"Mom, I want to be there," Megan said almost begging.

"Of course you will be there! I need you there."

Troy and Roy returned to Megan's room, and the women told them what they had decided.

"I'll pick ya up in the mornin' and take ya," Roy told May. "It's gettin' late, though, and both you girls need some rest. Do ya wanna go to the ranch tonight, or would ya rather stay at a motel tonight?"

"I'd rather not make that long drive to the ranch tonight, and I'd rather not be that far away from Megan," May answered.

"That's what I figured. Tell your youngin' 'night, and I'll getcha settled in a motel then."

They said their good-byes and Roy turned to Troy, "Are ya comin'?"

"No. The nurse said I could sleep here in the recliner. I'd rather not leave Megan alone right now."

"Suit yourself." Under his breath Roy said, "You'll do as ya please no matter what I say anyway!"

"Uh, Dad," Troy said as Roy and May reached the door, "you're the one with the hearin' problem, I'm not."

"And I'm also the one that chooses to ignore ill-mannered brats!" Roy teased back.

As they left the hospital, they met Bob Benson. He reeked of alcohol as usual, and Roy contemplated just walking on past him. Bob wasn't going to allow this, however. He stopped directly in front of them.

"Who's yer lady friend, Roy?" he asked pointing his thumb at May and giving Roy a toothless grin. "I ain't never seen her on the street before. Maybe you'll put a good word in for me."

Roy was furious! May extended her hand to Bob and said, "Hello, Bob. It's been awhile, but I remember you. I am May, Edna Gilliam's youngest daughter. What brings you way over here tonight?"

Bob was near tears and had trouble speaking. "I'm sorry, Miss May, 'bout talkin' like that. I was jist givin' ol' Roy here a hard time. I knew ya weren't no lady of the night. Anyone can tell by lookin' that you're a real lady. I've got a friend in the hospital that I'm a visitin'."

"That's all right, Bob. I knew you were just teasing Roy," May smiled sweetly at Bob.

"I was right fond of yer ma, yanno. I was mighty sorry for her passin'!"

"Yes, I know you were, Bob. It was good to see you again. You take care of yourself, and I hope your friend gets well soon," she said as Roy began walking away.

"Yes'm, Miss May. 'Twas good aseein' you again," Bob shouted after them.

"Why didn'tcha just invite 'im to come for supper sometime soon?" Roy exploded at May.

May stopped short, removed her hand from Roy's, and put both hands on her hips.
"*My temper's gone and dun it now,*" Roy thought as he took a step away from May. He was taking no chances on getting slapped or kicked, although in his heart he knew he deserved them both.

"How dare you, Roy Devon Brown! Who do you think you are talking to me in such a manner?"

"I'm sorry, May," Roy apologized sincerely. "You didn't deserve that. It's just that he made me so mad, and you were so cotton-pickin' sweet to 'im!"

"Did you ever stop to think that we might need him sometime in the future?"

"For what? I can't imagine Bob ever bein' any help to anyone. He can't stay sober long enuff to open a door fer ya."

"Maybe not, but he spent a lot of time with Mother. He may have some information that would be helpful."

"I'll give ya the benefit of the doubt. Can we be friends again?"

"We never stopped being friends, silly," May said as they began walking hand-in-hand again.

Roy drove May to the motel and helped her with her luggage. After she was settled, he headed home to sleep for the little bit of night that was left.

The next morning he was back at the motel early. To his surprise, May was up, dressed, and walking around the courtyard. He stopped the car and walked over to her, ignoring the sign telling everyone to "keep off the grass."

"I figured bein' a city gal you'd still be sleepin'," he said as he approached.

"And I figured you bein' a man of the law you could read signs," she said mocking his accent.

"I quit readin' signs when I retired," he grinned. "I thought maybe I could interest ya in some breakfast and goin' to see Megan before we get down to the business of diggin' up graves."

"Oh, that sounds wonderful, Roy. I do hope Megan had a good night and gets to leave the hospital today."

Roy and May tried to relax over breakfast, but they were both dreading the task ahead of them. An exhumation was never easy, and they almost feared what the autopsy would uncover. When they had finished eating the little their stomachs would tolerate due to their anxiety, they headed for the hospital.

May insisted on walking from the parking lot with Roy instead of getting out at the front door. Roy was surprised at how empty the parking lot was. He had never been to the hospital this early. He parked as close to the front door as possible, helped May out of the car, and locked the doors. May was so eager to see her daughter that she walked ahead knowing Roy was a faster walker and would soon catch up with her. As Roy turned from the car and started walking toward May, a tan car came speeding at her. Roy began running, but knew he'd never reach her in time to prevent the car from striking her!

Chapter Eight

May saw the speeding car just in time to jump to safety behind a parked car. As the tan car sped past Roy, he instinctively grabbed the pen from his shirt pocket and jotted down the tag number on the palm of his hand. His undivided attention then turned to May who was lying on the pavement next to the parked car.

As he ran to her side, she slowly reached for her purse.

"Pills," she whispered as Roy reached her side.

Roy opened her purse and found the nitroglycerin pills she needed. He put one in her mouth and yelled for a nurse who was walking toward the hospital. The nurse rushed over, felt May's pulse, and told her to lie quietly until she returned with help.

The nurse was back in record time with two other nurses and a gurney. They gingerly lifted May onto the gurney and headed to the emergency entrance. Roy was asked to wait in the waiting room while the doctor examined May. It seemed like an eternity before the doctor came out of the examining room to talk to Roy.

"Your friend will be fine. I would suggest no more excitement for a few days, but, as long as she keeps her pills handy, she shouldn't have any problems. If she needs me, please do not hesitate to call," he said handing Roy a business card.

"Are you gonna keep her in the hospital, or can she leave?" Roy asked.

"I don't think it will be necessary to admit her. She should be dressed and ready to leave shortly."

The doctor hurried down the hall and Roy was about to return to his seat when May came through the door. They walked hand-in-hand toward Megan's room.

"I'd rather Megan not know about that careless driver," May instructed Roy.

"That was not a careless driver. He or she deliberately tried to run you down and both the kids should be told. I got the tag number, and I want Troy to run it through the DMV to determine who the owner is," Roy replied.

May was surprised by his response. "You don't think it was an accident?"

"No way."

"But nobody knows I'm here except the kids and you."

Roy thought for a moment, and then he replied, "And Bob Benson!"

"Why in the world would Bob want to run me down, Roy? I think you're imagining things."

"Well, we'll see what the kids think," he said as they entered Megan's room.

The moment Megan saw May, she knew something was terribly wrong.

"What has happened, Mom?" she asked as Troy rose and indicated that May should sit in the comfortable recliner.

May smiled at Troy as she sat down. Roy moved the straight backed chair beside her and took her hand as he settled himself in it.

"I was involved in what I think was an accident on my way into the hospital," May began. "Roy seems to think it was no accident," she continued as she squeezed his hand and smiled at him.

They took turns telling what had happened and answering questions. Troy sat on the bed beside Megan and took her hand. She had turned very pale, and he was concerned about the impact this news might make on her recovery.

"Do you need the nurse?" he asked.

"No, I'm fine. This is just rather shocking. Who knew you were in town besides those of us in this room, Mom?" she asked regaining her composure.
"Only Bob Benson. We met him as we were leaving the hospital last night," replied May.

"You saw Bob outside this hospital?" Troy asked in disbelief. "What in the world was he doin' here? Was he sober? Did you talk to 'im?"

Troy was firing questions at May so quickly she didn't have a chance to respond to any of them.

"Slow down, son," Roy instructed. "Give May a chance to answer a question before you ask another one. If I remember the questions correctly, the answers are yes, he said he had a friend in the hospital; of course he wasn't sober; and only for a short time."
Roy's response made everyone laugh and eased the tension in the room.

"I wonder who his friend is?" Troy mused. "I think I'll go check the hospital roster and see if I recognize a name."

"While you're at it, would you call dispatch and have 'em run this license plate number?" Roy asked as he jotted the number written on his palm on a napkin lying on Megan's table.

"Do you mean you got the license on the tan car and you're just now tellin' me this bit of news? You're incorrigible, Dad!" Troy scolded as he snatched the napkin from his hand.

Megan loved the playful banter between father and son. Although they could sound quite angry at each other, one could feel the love between them. She now knew where Troy got his twinkling blue eyes. They were a mirror image of Roy's.

Troy stomped off toward the door, but, as he started to open it, he turned and walked back to Megan's bed. He bent and kissed her on the cheek.

"I won't be gone long," he grinned at her.

With that he left the room and headed outside to call the dispatcher on his cell phone. He gave the dispatcher the license number and said he'd call back in thirty minutes. He then headed toward the information desk to check the patient roster. He read the names on the roster five times just in case he'd missed one that he should recognize. He was disappointed to have to admit to himself that the only name he recognized on that roster was Megan's.

Troy went back outside to call the dispatcher, hoping he would have better luck with this lead.

"Don, did ya get a name and address on that license?" he asked when the dispatcher answered the phone.

"I got a name, but figured ya know the address," Don replied disinterested.

"Well?" asked Troy.
"Getting information out of Don is like pulling a lion's teeth!" he said to himself.

Don finally gave Troy the information he needed, and Troy raced back to Megan's room to tell everyone what he'd discovered.

When Troy entered the room, the doctor had just completed his examination of Megan and was giving the nurse discharge instructions. Megan smiled up at Troy with a beaming face knowing she would soon be out of that hospital bed.

Roy and May stated they would meet their children at Troy's house so both women could rest comfortably while they all talked and tried to make some sense out of the information they had.

"Dad, would you call Viola and see if she'd be willin' to come to my house, too? She's been tryin' to help us with this little mystery, and she was awfully worried 'bout Megan."

"Of course, son. I think that is a grand idea."

They both hugged Megan good-bye and left. While Megan dressed, Troy went to get the car and bring it to the front door. The entire time he was in the parking lot, he kept his eyes peeled for the tan car and for anyone he might recognize. Megan settled in the front seat beside him, and they pulled out of the parking lot without incident.

Once they left the congestion of the city behind, Troy relaxed and slipped his arm around Megan's shoulders. She instinctively snuggled closer and rested her head on his shoulder. She still had a terrible headache, but the doctor said that was to be expected. And, snuggling into Troy, she felt safe and more relaxed than she had in days. She hated to break the mood, but her curiosity could take it no longer.

"Any luck with Bob's friend?" she inquired.

"None at all. Your name was the only one I recognized. I'm considerin' questionin' 'im on the matter."

"Do you think now is the time to do that?"

"I dunno. That's one of the things I want to discuss when we're all together."

"What about the license number?" she prodded.

"Yes, I know who owns the car," he said, deliberately not telling Megan what he had discovered.

"Well, tell me who it is, and then we'll both know!"

"Not until we're all together. I want to see everyone's reaction at once."

"And you have the nerve to call your dad 'incorrigible'?" Megan exclaimed.

She knew Troy well enough to know that wild horses couldn't drag the name out of him, so she settled back down and was soon napping on his shoulder.

When they arrived at the house, Viola's car was already in the driveway beside Roy's. Megan roused as soon as Troy turned the car off. Troy turned and gave her a lingering kiss before he removed the keys from the ignition.

"I've really missed that!" he grinned down at her.

"Best medicine for what ails me," she replied.

They walked arm-in-arm to the house. Megan was weaker than she had realized, and she was glad for Troy's supporting arm. When they entered the house, they could hear laughter coming from the living room. They joined the trio just as another round of laughter erupted.

"What's so funny?" Troy asked.

"Oh, we were just relivin' the good ol' days," answered Viola. She immediately rose and hurried to Megan's side. After hugging her, she gestured toward the sofa where they had already prepared a bed for Megan to rest.

"Oh, I don't need to lie down," Megan protested. "I've been lying in bed for what seems like months. I'd rather sit up, but thank you for being so thoughtful," she added quickly. The last thing she wanted to do was hurt this dear lady's feelings.

"Suit yerself," Viola grinned. "Most youngin's do as they please anyway," she winked knowingly at May.

Troy and Megan both relaxed on the sofa, his arm around her with her leg tucked under her.

"I've got some interestin' news for yawl," Troy began. "Is everyone ready for this meetin' of the minds?"

Everyone nodded and encouraged Troy to reveal what he had discovered.

Chapter Nine

Troy took his arm from around Megan and scooted to the edge of the sofa. Megan could sense he was now in "sheriff" mode, and she sat up straight so she wouldn't be leaning on him and distract his thoughts. Troy reached for her hand and draped her arm across his knee as though he needed contact with her for strength and clarity. He then reached into his pocket and took out a small notebook. The edges of the book were worn from use. He flipped the pages until he came to the one he wanted, and then he began.

"Accordin' to Doc Reed, Grammy was poisoned to death. We know that Megan was bludgeoned, and now someone attempted to run May down. Folks, we have a cold-blooded killer in our midst!"

Viola shuffled in her chair at the mention of Grammy and appeared quite nervous. Troy realized she must feel somewhat uneasy since she was the last person to see Grammy alive, so he tried to put her at ease.

"Let me clarify that. When I say 'midst,' I am not meanin' anyone in this room. I fully trust everyone here!"

With that Viola's tension seemed to ease somewhat, but Troy sensed something was still bothering her. He made a mental note to try to talk to her alone. Maybe there was something she knew that she didn't want to divulge to the entire group.

"I know the identity of the owner of the tan car that tried to run May down, but I'm not sure how he fits into all this," Troy continued.

"Well, if you'd share that information with us, maybe we could help ya out!" Roy interjected.

"The car is registered to Jake Muntz," Troy confided.

Everyone was surprised by this revelation, and the room was quiet while they all thought about how this fit in with what they knew.

"It was not Jake drivin': The driver was shorter with longer hair. I think it was a woman," Roy finally said breaking the silence.

"Ethel?" Troy asked.

Hearing her daughter-in-law's name caused Viola to turn pale. She couldn't imagine Ethel being a killer.
"I dunno, possibly," answered Roy.

"Surely not, Ethel," Viola said defensively. "She didn't even know May was in town!" she reminded them.

"That's what has me puzzled," said Troy. "No one knew except Bob Benson. How is Bob connected to the driver of that car? This just doesn't make any sense."

Megan had been very quiet mulling this new information over mentally.

"I think we need to start at the beginning and the pieces will fall into place," she said. "Mom, first thing tomorrow, you need to make the necessary arrangements to have Grammy's body exhumed and an autopsy run."

"What? Land sakes, girl, have ya gone bonkers from that hit on the noodle?" Viola exclaimed not believing her ears. "Edna should be allowed to rest peacefully!"

"I'm sorry if this offends you, Viola but I agree with Megan," May said patting Viola on the knee. "We need to know the truth behind Mama's death before we can make sense of any of this. I certainly don't think Mama would mind if it saves someone else's life!"

"I'm not so sure about that, but do as ya please," Viola responded. "I'm afraid this has been a bit too much for me. If yawl don't mind, I'd like to go home and lock myself in my room for the rest of the night. I don't think I can be of much help right now anyway. I'm just too upset."

"I was gonna suggest May and Megan stay here tonight. Would you like to stay, too?" Troy offered.

"That would be great, but Ethel would be suspicious if I didn't return home. If what you say is true, I wouldn't wanna cause her to go on no killin' spree!"

"I don't think it would come to that, but perhaps yer right," Troy grinned at her. "Before ya go, what can ya tell us about Ethel's past or her family?"

"Not much, really. When David had to go overseas to fight, she came to live with me 'cause she had no parents livin'. She just stayed after he was killed. She met and married Jake, and he moved in with me, too."

"I see. Well, thanks for your help. Are you sure you're up to drivin' home?"

"Yeah, I'll be fine. I'll talk to yawl tomorrow," Viola said as she hugged each of the women good-bye.

"Promise you'll call me if you feel like yer in any danger or if anyone over there's actin' strange, okay?" Troy said as he walked her to the door.

"Oh, don't worry yer handsome lil' head; you'll be the first one I call!" she said patting his chest in her usual flirtatious manner.

Troy returned to the living room, plopped down beside Megan, and drew her close to him. He was visibly upset by the impact this situation had on Viola. He truly cared about her and wanted to protect her. He felt he had failed his beloved Grammy, and he didn't want to fail Viola, too.

Megan wished she knew what to say to make Troy feel better, but she didn't seem able to think of anything. May rose from her chair and perched her small frame on the arm of the sofa with one hand on Troy's back.

"Troy, Viola's a lot tougher than you give her credit for being. Never underestimate her; she'll probably be the one to clear all this up," she added with a chuckle. "Now, I think we need to feed my daughter, or she'll never regain her strength."

This statement brought Troy out of his black thoughts. "Oh, I'm so sorry. I bet yer starvin', Megan," he said hugging her.

"Well, Mother knows best," Megan grinned.

"I'll run to the diner and get the 'family feast' to go. That should fill us all up," he replied.

"If ya don't mind goin by yerself, I'll stay here and take care of the women," Roy said as he stood and tried to look like a he-man.

"I'm sure I can handle this alone," Troy answered.

"Our mighty protector can show me where things are, and we'll set the table while you're gone," May teased Roy.

Troy kissed Megan good-bye, grabbed his keys off the table by the door, and headed for town. He didn't plan on being gone long, but, as he stopped at a stop sign, he noticed Viola's car parked at the library.

"I thought she was goin' straight home," he said to himself. "Wonder what's goin' on?"

He pulled into a parking slot beside Viola's car and headed toward the library. Before he reached the door, Viola came strolling toward her car. She seemed flustered when she saw Troy, but there was no way to avoid him.

"Are ya okay?" he inquired.

"Oh, yes, I feel much better," she replied. "I hadn't talked to my friend, Edith, today, so I just stopped to chat with her a bit. She's comin' to see me. I'm so excited!"

"Really?" Troy said, intrigued.

It seemed strange that this mystery woman would come to visit right after Viola had gotten so upset. He felt there was more there than met the eye.

"When?" he asked.

"Her plane will arrive in Amarillo tomorrow evenin'. Would you, by any chance, care to drive me over to meet her?"

"Sure, I'd be glad to. Mind if Megan comes along if she's up to it?"

"Uh, I really think it would be better if it was jist you and me," Viola stammered. "Edith's kinda shy when meetin' folks," she quickly added.

"No problem. Megan needs to rest, anyway," he replied, puzzled by Viola's reaction at the mention of Megan going.

Viola seemed relieved that she hadn't upset Troy. "I'll meet ya here at the library at five o'clock tomorrow then. Okay?"

"Why don'tcha come out to the house. It's right on the way to the airport, and your car won't be left on Main Street unattended tomorrow when the teenagers hit town for their Friday night shenanigans," Troy suggested.

"I swear, you think like a cop all the time!" Viola teased. "I'll be at your house a little after five then. That'll gimme a chance to see my Angel again real quick before we leave."

"Okay, then, see ya tomorrow. Go home and rest now," he said as he helped her into her car. Viola smiled and waved as she backed out into the street without looking behind her and drove off.

Troy got into his car and drove to the diner. As he waited for the food, he thought about the day's events.

"Things just keep gettin' stranger!" he thought. *"But the sun will still come up tomorrow!"* he quoted Grammy with a smile.

When Troy returned home with the food, he found his guests sitting in the kitchen at a fully set table talking. He stood in the doorway for a moment taking a mental picture of the people who meant the most to him sitting in his kitchen so cozily. Roy was the first to notice him.

"What's yer problem, boy? We're starvin' here, and yer just standin' there lettin' the vittles get cold!"

Troy laughed and set the food on the counter. He and Megan dished the food into bowls and onto platters and set it on the table. They had an enjoyable dinner talking about everything except the mystery that had brought them together. When they were finished, Roy and May insisted on cleaning the kitchen and putting the leftovers away while Troy and Megan relaxed in the living room.

They were just getting settled on the sofa when the doorbell rang.

"Who could that be at this hour?" Troy wondered.

He went to the door and Megan could hear him talking to another man. Troy soon returned carrying Megan's camera.

"That was Don, from the office. The sheriff asked him to bring your camera by to me on his way home. He said there was only one picture on it and the sheriff wants me to put it on my computer and check out the reflection in the window."

"But I didn't take any pictures. I was hit when I started to take the first one."

"All I know is what I was just told. Let's check it out," Troy said as he pulled an armchair beside his computer chair.

Megan sat in the armchair and leaned toward the computer screen while Troy connected the camera to the computer. He pushed some buttons, and a blurry picture of Megan's car appeared on the screen.

"You must've pushed the button as you fell," Troy explained. "You said you were fixin' to take a picture when ya got hit. Your reflexes must've pushed the button although you weren't aware of it."

Megan sat mesmerized as Troy zoomed into the reflection in the window. As he instructed the computer to clean the image up, Roy and May joined them. Troy told them what they were doing. As the computer worked, they all stared at the image on the monitor. Suddenly the screen went blank and then a picture of Ethel holding a board aimed at the back of Megan's head appeared on the screen. There was an intake of breath, and Megan turned deathly white. She couldn't believe her eyes.

"Why would Ethel want to harm me? I've done nothing to her! Was she driving the car that tried to run my mother down?"

Troy turned the computer off, turned toward Megan, and took both her hands in his. He was worried; her color was bad.

"Let's go back to the couch," he said softly.

They all returned to the sitting area, and Troy held Megan in his arms.

"We still don't know the 'why,' but we know the 'who,'" he stated. "We know Ethel is the one who hit you, and, more than likely, was the one who tried to run May down since Jake owns the car, both of which are attempted murder. Tomorrow we'll get an autopsy on Grammy, and then I'll bring Ethel in for questionin' for murder."

"How did Ethel know I was in town, though?" asked May.

"I dunno, but there must be some connection between her and Bob."

The foursome sat and talked into the night. Troy gave Megan her medicine, and she slowly began to relax in his arms. Roy showed May to a guest room and bid her goodnight. When Roy returned to the living room, Troy had leaned his head on the back of the sofa and was snoring. Roy didn't bother him but turned out the lights, locked the door, and retired to a guest room between the living room and May's room. He wasn't sure what might happen during the few hours left until morning, and he wanted to be in a position to protect everyone. He fell asleep with his hand resting on his revolver that lay on the nightstand beside his bed.

The night passed without incident, and everyone awoke to the smell of coffee, bacon, and eggs. Megan was the first to arrive in the kitchen because she had slept in her clothes. There she found Troy with a kitchen towel tied around his waist to protect his slacks from splatters.

"Ummmm, sure smells good," she said as she wrapped her arms around his waist and kissed the back of his neck.

"Keep doin' that and I'll cook every meal," he replied, handing her a steaming cup of coffee. "I thought we should all eat a hardy breakfast with the big day we have ahead of us," he explained.

"You think of everything!" she complimented.

They were soon joined by Roy and May who were as surprised as Megan had been. When they had devoured the delicious breakfast, Troy shooed the other three off to shower and dress so they could get to the sheriff's office early. As they kept the two bathrooms busy, Troy stacked the dirty dishes into the dishwasher. When the kitchen was back in order, he went to his room to finish dressing. When he returned to the living room, everyone was standing with their arms folded, patting the floor with one foot, and looking at the clock. Troy burst out laughing that contagious laugh, and, soon, all four were cleansing their spirits with laughter.

"Well, let's go!" Troy ordered as the laughter finally died down.

When they arrived at the sheriff's office, the sheriff told them it usually took awhile for such a request to be granted.

"An autopsy should have been performed without a family member requesting one under the circumstances!" Megan was practically yelling at the sheriff.

"What circumstances?" the sheriff asked innocently.

"You know very well what circumstances," Megan retorted and she flung the death certificate on his desk.

The sheriff picked up the paper and read it.

"Okay, I didn't realize you'd seen this. You are right. An autopsy should've been performed, but the law states that a family member must request one. We had no right to do it without someone's request because it appeared to be an accidental death. Doc didn't fill this out until after the funeral. Under the circumstances, I'm sure we can cut through some of the red tape and get this done sooner."

Megan thanked him and settled down to wait with the others. The sheriff got a form from a file cabinet and took it and a notepad to the secretary. He then returned to his office and sat down behind his desk.

"Would yawl like sumthin' to drink while we wait?" he asked as he picked his own cup up and took a drink of hot coffee.

Everyone declined stating they had just had breakfast. This conversation had barely ended when the secretary came in carrying the form and the notepad.

"Here ya go, Sheriff. Sorry it took me so long, but I had to change the ribbon in my typewriter."
Megan looked at her in amazement. She wondered if the sheriff knew how lucky he was to have such an efficient employee. She doubted it.

"Not to worry, Sue. I jist now got ready for it," the sheriff said with a wink.

Sue blushed and quickly returned to her desk and began typing on something else.

"We couldn't make it without Sue, could we, Troy?" the sheriff asked seriously.

"You can say that again, sir. I just hope she never realizes just how good she is 'cause we couldn't afford her then," he added with a chuckle.

The sheriff nodded in agreement as he rose from his chair, and Megan had to admit to herself that she had been wrong.

"I'll be back as soon as I get the judge to sign this," he said shaking the form Sue had just brought to him.

It seemed as though the sheriff had been gone an eternity to the four people waiting in his office, but he was actually only gone the better part of three

_Time and again I have searched for you, not
knowing that it was me I needed to find._
        —Betty MacDonald

We may have spent many years looking for the
partner who would complete our lives. We were
certain that happiness was guaranteed when the
search culminated in the perfect selection. How
tragic it seems when we discover that happiness
still eludes us. The search, coupled with the belief
that someone else is our ticket to happiness, has
lead us down many dark alleys.

We are learning now that finding our true self
offers us the wholeness we thought would come
from our attachment to another person. The Steps
will guide our self-discovery. Through the Steps,
the meetings we attend, and the friends we make,
we'll find our real self. Knowing her fully, accept-
ing her completely, will fill the void we thought
only another person could fill.

_I will pay attention to who I am today. I will honor
the whole of me. I know genuine happiness can be
found only in this way._

hours. He rushed into his office waving a paper in his hand and grinning from ear to ear.

"Come on, folks. The gravedigger's waitin' on us, and he's ready to go to lunch!"

The foursome jumped to their feet and hurried out of the office following the sheriff. Everything seemed surreal to Megan who had been dozing, and Troy had to guide her to the car.

"Are you up to doin' this, Megan?" he asked as he helped her into the car.

"Absolutely. I want to finally find out how my Grammy died!"

Troy knew it would do no good to try to talk her or May into staying in the car, so he didn't try when they arrived. The sheriff handed the man who managed the cemetery the form and told his employees to begin. Before long Grammy's casket sat on the grass in front of them. Megan moved toward the casket slowly and gingerly touched the lid with shaking hands.

"Hold on there, missy," a man getting out of a van shouted at her. "I'm the county coroner and nobody's openin' that box but me. And I ain't openin' it out here. It'll hafta be taken to the morgue, and then I'll inspect the remains."

The man had walked right past Megan and seemed to be talking to the sheriff during the last of his statement. The sheriff held up a finger to Megan indicating he would talk to her in a minute. The casket was loaded into the coroner's van, and he drove off toward town without another word.

"I've instructed Mac not to open the casket until we are present. Judge Pierce wrote those instructions on the bottom of the form he signed. He wants witnesses to verify no funny business has transpired since the exhumation. I'm sure you noticed that a deputy went with Mac to make sure the judge's instructions are followed to the letter."

"Thank you for all that you have done. I appreciate it so much," Megan said as she extended her hand to him.

"No problem, ma'am. I'm glad I could help. Troy, when yawl are finished at the morgue, would you tell George he can go to lunch?"

"Of course," Troy replied as they all turned to go to his car.

When they arrived at the morgue, May looked very pale.

"Honey, I think I'll sit here in the lobby while you handle this, if you don't mind," she told Megan. "I just don't think I can handle seeing Mama like that."

"Oh, Mother, I'm so sorry! I never realized how hard this must be on you. Are you sure you'll be all right out here?"

"I'll stay with her," Roy interjected as he sat in a chair beside May.

"Thank you, Roy. You are such a dear man," Megan said as she kissed the top of his head.

Troy and Megan continued down the long hall hand-in-hand. When they saw Mac, they entered the room. Troy nodded to Mac, and he began trying to open the casket lid.

"It seems to be stuck," Mac told George who had walked up beside him.

"It was locked," Troy informed them.

"Why in the world would anyone lock a casket?" Mac asked unbelievingly. "I ain't never heerd of such a thing in all my born days!"

George pulled a pocketknife from his uniform pocket and patiently began trying to pick the lock. Suddenly they all heard a click, and the lid swung open. Megan let out a gasp, and Troy feared she would faint as the contents of the casket were revealed.

"There ain't no way I can perform an autopsy on that!" exclaimed Mac.

Chapter Ten

Troy told George he could go to lunch and he'd call the sheriff and inform him of the findings. He then put an arm around Megan's waist and slowly walked her back down the long corridor to the lobby. He motioned to Roy to follow and walked to the car. Once they were all inside and he had the air conditioner turned on high, he turned in his seat so he could see Roy and May.

"Yer not gonna believe this," he said shaking his head. "I saw it, and I don't even believe it."

"For heaven's sake, Troy, tell us what has happened! Megan looks as if she's seen a ghost!" Roy scolded his son.

"Nope, no ghost. Jist a casket full o' rocks!" Troy said to their disbelief. "I told ya you weren't gonna believe it!"

"Rocks?" May said as though she had never heard the word before.

"Rocks," Troy repeated. "Now I know why the casket was locked, but where is Grammy?"

"Who would do such a cruel thing?" May asked. "There's no telling where my poor, poor Mama's body is."

May was now sobbing uncontrollably and tears were streaming down Megan's face. Troy turned the car toward home and began punching numbers on his cell phone.

"This is Troy Brown, and I need to talk to Doc Reed now. I've got an emergency!" he said into the phone. "Well, find 'im immediately and tell 'im to come to my house and to hurry. I've got two women here that may both die from heart attacks if he doesn't get here soon!"

With that he snapped the phone shut and sped the car up. They arrived at his house in record time, and he and Roy helped the women out of the car and into the house.

"I want to stay with Mother," Megan told Troy.

"I figured that," he said taking her into May's room.

Megan curled next to her mother with her head on May's shoulder. May automatically put her arm around her daughter as she had done so many times when Megan was a child. As Roy went to the closet to get a quilt for them, Troy whispered to him that he needed to make a call to the sheriff. Roy nodded, covered mother and daughter with the quilt, and settled himself in a chair nearby.

Troy sat at his desk and, with a sigh, dialed the phone.

"We got a problem, boss," he said as soon as the sheriff answered.

"So I hear," the sheriff replied. "George came on back to the office instead of goin' to eat. How's yer women folks doin'?"

"They are both in shock. I've called for Doc Reed to come see 'bout 'em but haven't heard from 'im yet."

"I saw 'im leave town headin' in yer direction jist a bit ago. He should be out there soon."

"That's good news. Now, whatcha gonna do 'bout this other mess?"

"I sent George out to bring Ethel in for questionin'. Everything seems to come back to her, and I want some answers!"

"Let me know how that goes, will ya?"

"Yeah, although yer supposed to be on vacation!"

Troy grinned. "It's been an interestin' vacation."

The sheriff laughed and said, "I'll keep ya up to snuff, Troy."

Troy had just hung up the phone when his front door burst open and Viola rushed in.

"What's happened? Has sumthin' happened to my Angel? Where is everyone?" she shouted.

Troy went to the foyer to try to calm Viola down. As he opened his mouth to speak to her, Doc Reed came through the open door shutting it behind him.

"Is this the patient?" Doc asked.

"No, they are in the guest room, and you have some explainin' to do, Doc," Troy said as he led the way to the bedroom. "They have had a bad shock at the morgue today, and I think you know more about it than you're tellin'," he continued.

"Oh dear," Viola said shaking her head. "You're needed here, Troy. I'll just go to the airport by myself."

"The airport," Troy repeated. "I'm sorry, Viola, I completely forgot about picking up your friend."

"Yes, my friend, Edith Guthrie, from Florida," Viola elaborated.

Doc Reed smiled at the old lady. He certainly didn't want her driving to the airport alone.
"No tellin' how many accidents she'd cause," he thought to himself.

"Troy, you're right. I do have some explainin' to do. You take Viola to get her friend, and I'll stay here and tend to the women. When yawl get back, I'll tell ya everything I know," Doc said as they entered the bedroom.

"I'm not goin' anywhere 'til I know they're gonna be okay," Troy said gesturing toward the two women cuddled under the quilt.

Doc immediately listened to May's heart and was pleased with the steady rhythm. She and Megan were both in shock, but it apparently hadn't affected her heart. He felt somewhat responsible for what had happened to them and was glad they weren't any worse than they were.

Doc turned to Troy, "They're gonna be just fine. You run along and let me work my magic. Your dad will be here to help me."

Troy, just like a child, looked to his dad for approval. Roy nodded, and Troy rounded the bed to tell Megan good-bye.

"I've gotta be gone awhile, Megan. Viola needs me to drive her to the airport to get her friend. Will you be okay with Doc Reed and Dad?"

Megan smiled up at Troy, "Quit worrying about me. I'll be just fine."

Troy bent to kiss her cheek, but she turned her head to receive a proper kiss. Right now she didn't care who was watching; she needed the reassurance his kiss gave her.

"Hurry back," she said as he turned to leave.
"You can count on that!" he said over his shoulder.

Viola was full of questions about the events of the day, and the trip to the airport passed quickly as Troy tried to answer all of them. She was still asking questions as he parked the car and walked the short distance to the terminal. Troy was relieved to see that the flight from Miami was on schedule. The announcement stating that the passengers were now leaving the plane had just come across the loud speaker when Troy's phone began to ring.

"You go on and meet your friend. I've gotta take this call. I'll wait right here for yawl," he instructed Viola.

Troy had turned his back to the people hurrying past and didn't see Viola when she returned with Edith.

"Troy, this is my friend Edith," Viola said to his back.

Troy turned with his lopsided grin and his hand extended ready to meet Edith. The moment he saw her, he turned deathly white and had trouble breathing!

Chapter Eleven

Troy regained his composure fairly quickly, grabbed Edith around the waist with both arms, and began swinging her in circles.

"Put me down, you hooligan!" she said as she hit the top of his head with her purse.

"Grammy! I can't believe my eyes!" he said finally letting her feet touch the floor but still hugging her tight. "We all thought you were dead! I attended your funeral!"

"I will be dead if ya don't let me go so I can breathe!" Grammy playfully scolded him.

"You have no idea the trouble you have caused," he scolded back.

"Yes, I do. Viola has kept me informed daily by the computer," Grammy said apologetically. "That's why I'm here now. I hoped to arrive before yawl dug me up, but this was the first flight available."

"Let's retrieve your luggage, and you can fill me in on the way to my house. There are a couple of ladies there that need to see ya. I just hope the sight of ya doesn't make May have a heart attack!" Troy said as he guided the two women through the crowd.

At the baggage counter, Troy grabbed the three large suitcases that Grammy said were hers. Even with his load, he had to slow his pace so the elderly women could keep up as they walked to the car.

"Ladies, we really need to hurry as much as possible. The sheriff called while we were at the airport, and he's gonna come to the house to talk to us. I'd like for May and Megan to have a little time to adjust to the fact that you're not dead before he arrives," Troy said in an attempt to speed the women's pace.

"You're such a worrywart," Viola replied. "Doc Reed will have already told them everything, and they'll be waitin' with open arms for Grammy's arrival!" she continued.

"Doc knew your friend was actually Grammy?" Troy asked.

"Of course he did! How else did ya think we pulled this off?" Grammy asked. "After Doc discovered someone was poisonin' me, this was the only way we could be sure I'd be safe. I talked to May and Megan at least twice a week, and I knew they'd find out who had killed me. All I had to do was die! I did that with the help of Viola and Doc Reed," she proudly explained.

"If Megan and I had done sumthin' like that, you'd be turnin' us both over your knee!" Troy scolded.

Neither lady said a word, and they both chose to sit in the back seat as Troy put the luggage in the trunk. He got in the car shaking his head, and his phone began to ring.

"Saved by the bell," Grammy chuckled.

"Maybe not, it's Megan," Troy replied. "Hi, hon. Is everythin' okay?" he said into the phone.

"It is if the wild story Doc Reed just told us is true," Megan answered. "Is Viola's friend really Grammy, Troy?"

Megan held her breath as she waited for Troy's answer.

"Yes, Megan, Grammy is right here in the car with me. You should be able to hug her or turn her over your knee, whichever ya feel like, in about twenty-five minutes."

"Can I talk to her now?" Megan sobbed into the phone. "I just need to hear her voice to know it's true!"

Troy handed the phone to Grammy, "She needs to hear your voice."

"Megan, my angel child," Grammy said softly into the phone as tears began to stream down her face.

"Grammy! I don't know if I'm laughing or crying; I'm so happy! Tell Troy to get a move on!"

"I'll let you tell 'im, child. He won't listen to me," Grammy replied and handed the phone back to Troy.

"Megan, the sheriff called while we were at the airport, and he's comin' to the house to talk to us. He's been questionin' Ethel and says he has some answers for us."

"Oh good. Does he know about Grammy?"

"No, and neither does your Aunt Carol. Would you wanna call and see if she'd come to the house. We've kinda left her out of everythin', and I don't think that's fair to her. It sounds like she's been innocent in all of this."

"Oh, I've been so mean to her. I was sure she had something to do with Grammy's death! Of course, I'll call her. And, Troy?"

"Yes?"

"Thank you for all you've done!"

"I haven't done anythin', Megan. I've been just as confused as everyone else."

"You've been there for me through it all, and I love you for that!"

"Hold that thought 'til we're alone," Troy said softly into the phone.

Megan could feel the blush in her neck and was glad Troy couldn't see her.
"Roy's starting the coffee now, and I'll go throw some snacks together real quick. Hurry home, Troy," she said and snapped her phone shut as she hurried to the kitchen.

As Troy put his phone back in his shirt pocket, he began whistling. The two friends in the back seat quit their chatter and stared at him.

"Just what, may I ask, are your intentions where my granddaughter is concerned?" Grammy asked.

"Well, Grammy, ya can ask all ya want, but, until I ask her, I ain't tellin'," he said winking at Grammy in the rearview mirror.

"Well, I nevah!" Grammy huffed with a smile on her face.

As Troy pulled the car into the driveway, he saw that Carol was already there which pleased him. He turned off the engine and the lights and got out to help the ladies out of the car. Just as he opened Grammy's door, the door to the house opened and everyone came rushing out to the car.

Everyone was talking at once and hugging everyone, and Troy was still standing by the open car door with that lopsided grin on his face.

"You can shut the door, now," Megan said.

Troy snapped out of his trance and, laughing, shut the door. He put his arm around Megan's waist and guided her to the front porch.

"Yawl come on in," he shouted over the noise.

Everyone started toward the house just as the sheriff's car pulled into the drive. Grammy turned and walked over to the sheriff as he shut his car door.

"Your timin' has always been perfect, Sheriff," she said extending her hand to him.

"Well, now it ain't no wonder Ethel didn't know what had become of yer body, Ms. Gilliam," he said shaking her hand. "That was the only question I had left, and now it's answered as well!"

"Well, come on in and answer some questions for the rest of us."

Everyone settled in the kitchen where Roy had put paper plates and the snacks on the table. As soon as they all had their plates full and gotten their drinks, Troy asked the sheriff to enlighten them.

"I mainly wantcha all to know you can sleep safe tonight. I have booked Ethel Muntz into the city jail with two charges of attempted murder, which by the way, she has confessed to. She didn't know who you were, Miss Megan, but she thoughtcha were too nosy. She was afraid you'd found out about her poisonin' the old lady. Them's her words, not mine, Ms. Gilliam," he said apologetically.

"When she sent her brother to see if you were dead or in the hospital, he reported back that you were indeed still alive, and, when he saw your mother outside the hospital, he made the connection. That's when Ethel decided to either run over your mother or skeer her into havin' a heart attack. Either way, she'd be dead."

"Bob Benson is Ethel's brother?" Troy asked surprised.

"Yep, her baby brother," the sheriff answered between gulps of coffee.

"But who poisoned me?" Grammy wanted to know.

"Ethel. 'Cause of her brother."

"I don't understand," Megan said.

"Me either," replied Grammy and her two daughters at the same time.

"Well, since Bob had been such a help to you after the passin' of yer hubby, she thought for sure you'd give 'im some o' yer land. Instead, Carol came home to help ya make the place into a guest ranch. Y'awl sold most o' the land to finance the ranch in the beginnin' and, not only did ya not give any to Bob, ya didn't have a job for 'im anymore. She got it in her head that if you was outta the picture, Ms. Carol would need Bob's help again, so he'd at least have a job again. Folks get crazy notions, for sure."

"Then when Grammy and Viola faked her death, Bob thought Ethel had killed her, didn't he?" Troy asked.

"Yep. He still thinks that 'cause he don't know Ms. Gilliam's alive. He thought so highly of ya that he couldn't bear the thought of bein' the cause of yer death, ma'am," he said looking at Grammy. "That's why he started drinkin'."

Everyone had grown silent thinking of the destruction that Ethel's greed had caused. The sheriff looked at his watch and hurriedly drank the rest of his coffee.

"Land's, my wife's gonna skin me alive! I had no idea it was so late. If yawl don't have any more questions for me, I'll be headin' on home," he said picking up his hat.

Troy walked the sheriff to the front door thanking him for coming to explain everything to them.

"So I guess it's all over but the trial, huh?" he said as they reached the door.

"Yep. Now you can enjoy your last week of vacation," the sheriff said poking Troy in the ribs.

"That's exactly what I intend to do, too," Troy replied.

Troy returned to the kitchen where everyone was still sitting discussing what they had just been told. Troy looked at the clock hanging on the kitchen wall as he entered the room.

"I hate to break this up, but it's mighty late and everyone's had a busy day," he said.

Megan couldn't help herself. "The sun will still come up tomorrow," she quoted Grammy.

"That it will, but I won't be up to greet it if I don't lay these old bones down soon," Grammy chuckled.